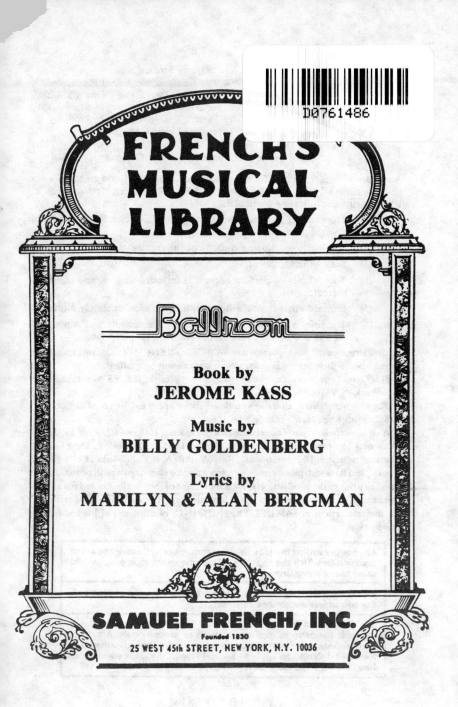

FRENCH'S MUSICAL LIBRARY

Ballroom

Book by
JEROME KASS

Music by
BILLY GOLDENBERG

Lyrics by
MARILYN & ALAN BERGMAN

SAMUEL FRENCH, INC.

Founded 1830
25 WEST 45th STREET, NEW YORK, N.Y. 10036

Amateurs wishing to arrange for the production of BALLROOM must make application to SAMUEL FRENCH, INC., at 25 West 45th Street, New York, N. Y.
10036, giving the following particulars:

(1) The name of the town and theatre or hall in which it is proposed to
     give the production.

(2) The maximum seating capacity of the theatre or hall.

(3) Scale of ticket prices.

(4) The number of performances it is intended to give, and the dates
     thereof.

(5) Indicate whether you will use an orchestration or simply a piano.

(6) The title, number of performances, gross receipts and amount of
     royalty and rental paid on your last musical performed.

Upon receipt of these particulars SAMUEL FRENCH, INC., will quote the
terms upon which permission for performances will be granted.

Stock royalty quoted on application to Samuel French, Inc., 25 West 45th Street,
New York, N.Y. 10036.

For all other rights than those stipulated above apply to The Lantz Office, Inc.,
888 Seventh Ave., New York, N.Y. 10106.

A set of orchestral parts consisting of Reed I, Reed II, Reed III, Reed IV, Horn,
Trumpets 1&2 (one book), Trumpet 3, Trombone 1, Trombone 2, Trombone 3,
Guitar, Percussion 1&2 (two books), Harp, Violins A, B, C, (3 books), Cello A&B (2
books), and Bass with piano conductor score and 20 chorus parts will be loaned two
months prior to the production ONLY on receipt of the royalty quoted for all performances, the rental fee and a refundable deposit. The deposit will be refunded
on the safe return to SAMUEL FRENCH, INC. of all material loaned for the
production.

Printed in U.S.A.

ISBN 0 573 68140 6

MAJESTIC THEATRE

⑤ A Shubert Organization Theatre

rald Schoenfeld, *Chairman*   Bernard B. Jacobs, *President*

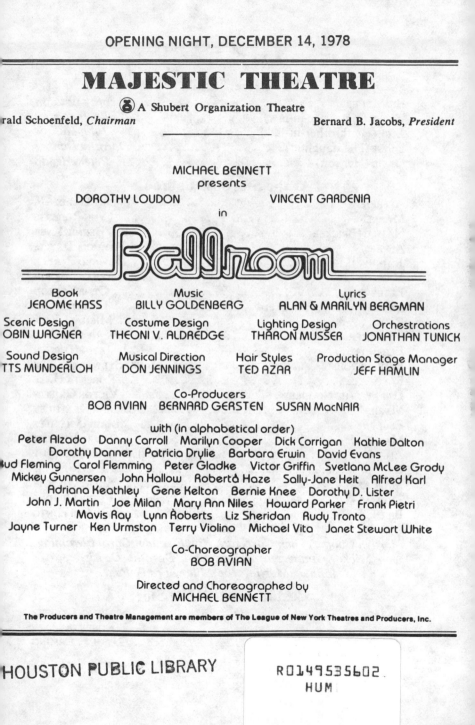

MICHAEL BENNETT
presents

DOROTHY LOUDON   VINCENT GARDENIA

in

Ballroom

Book	Music	Lyrics
JEROME KASS	BILLY GOLDENBERG	ALAN & MARILYN BERGMAN

Scenic Design	Costume Design	Lighting Design	Orchestrations
OBIN WAGNER	THEONI V. ALDREDGE	THARON MUSSER	JONATHAN TUNICK

Sound Design	Musical Direction	Hair Styles	Production Stage Manager
TTS MUNDERLOH	DON JENNINGS	TED AZAR	JEFF HAMLIN

Co-Producers
BOB AVIAN   BERNARD GERSTEN   SUSAN MacNAIR

with (in alphabetical order)

Peter Alzado   Danny Carroll   Marilyn Cooper   Dick Corrigan   Kathie Dalton
Dorothy Danner   Patricia Drylie   Barbara Erwin   David Evans
ud Fleming   Carol Flemming   Peter Gladke   Victor Griffin   Svetlana McLee Grody
Mickey Gunnersen   John Hallow   Robertå Haze   Sally-Jane Heit   Alfred Karl
Adriana Keathley   Gene Kelton   Bernie Knee   Dorothy D. Lister
John J. Martin   Joe Milan   Mary Ann Niles   Howard Parker   Frank Pietri
Mavis Ray   Lynn Roberts   Liz Sheridan   Rudy Tronto
Jayne Turner   Ken Urmston   Terry Violino   Michael Vita   Janet Stewart White

Co-Choreographer
BOB AVIAN

Directed and Choreographed by
MICHAEL BENNETT

The Producers and Theatre Management are members of The League of New York Theatres and Producers, Inc.

THE CAST

The Family

BEA ASHER .... *Dorothy Loudon*
HELEN (Her sister-in-law).................... *Sally-Jane Heit*
JACK (Her brother-in-law) .... *John Hallow*
DIANE (Her daughter)...................... *Dorothy Danner*
DAVID (Her son) .... *Peter Alzado*

At the Stardust Ballroom

ALFRED ROSSI .... VINCENT GARDENIA
MARLENE .... LYNN ROBERTS
NATHAN BRICKER .... BERNIE KNEE
ANGIE .... PATRICIA DRYLIE
JOHNNY "LIGHTFEET" .... HOWARD PARKER
MARTHA.................................. BARBARA ERWIN
PETEY .... GENE KELTON
SHIRLEY .... LIZ SHERIDAN
PAUL .... MICHAEL VITA
"SCOOTER"............................... DANNY CARROLL
ELEANOR .... JAYNE TURNER
PAULINE KRIM .... JANET STEWART WHITE
FAYE .... ROBERTA HAZE
HARRY "THE NOODLE" .... VICTOR GRIFFIN
MARIE .... ADRIANA KEATHLEY
EMILY .... MARY ANN NILES
MARIO .... TERRY VIOLINO
ANITRA........................... SVETLANA MCLEE GRODY
CARL .... DAVID EVANS
MARGARET .... MAVIS RAY
THOMAS .... PETER GLADKE
BILL .... RUDY TRONTO

And

*Marilyn Cooper, Dick Corrigan, Bud Fleming, Carol Flemming,
Mickey Gunnersen, Alfred Karl, Dorothy D. Lister,
John J. Martin, Joe Milan, Frank Pietri*

Customers at Bea's Store

NATALIE.................................. MARILYN COOPER
ESTELLE .... ROBERTA HAZE
KATHY .... CAROL FLEMMING

4

MUSICAL NUMBERS

A TERRIFIC BAND AND A REAL NICE CROWD ....
.... BEA ASHER
A SONG FOR DANCIN' .... THE BALLROOM REGULARS
.... SUNG BY: MARLENE AND NATHAN
ONE BY ONE .... ANGIE, LIGHTFEET, THE BALLROOM REGULARS
.... SUNG BY: MARLENE AND NATHAN
THE DANCE MONTAGE .... THE BALLROOM REGULARS
DREAMS .... MARLENE
SOMEBODY DID ALRIGHT FOR HERSELF .... BEA ASHER
THE TANGO CONTEST .... EMILY & MARIO, BEA & AL,
MARTHA & PETEY, ANITRA & CARL, SHIRLEY & PAUL,
MARGARET & THOMAS, MARIE & HARRY
GOODNIGHT IS NOT GOODBYE .. THE BALLROOM REGULARS
.... SUNG BY: MARLENE AND NATHAN
I'VE BEEN WAITING ALL MY LIFE ....
.... THE BALLROOM REGULARS
.... SUNG BY: NATHAN
I LOVE TO DANCE................. BEA ASHER AND AL ROSSI
MORE OF THE SAME .... THE BALLROOM REGULARS
.... SUNG BY: MARLENE AND NATHAN
FIFTY PERCENT .... BEA
THE STARDUST WALTZ .... THE BALLROOM REGULARS
I WISH YOU A WALTZ .... BEA

PLACE: The Bronx

TIME: The Present

**VOCAL SELECTIONS FROM BALLROOM
AVAILABLE FOR PURCHASE FROM
SAMUEL FRENCH, INC.**

Ballroom

BEA'S JUNK SHOP

HELEN *is at the counter, helping* NATALIE. ESTELLE *is browsing.*

NATALIE. (*Holding up object.*) Oh, this is a lovely piece.
HELEN. Isn't it?
NATALIE. What is it, crystal?
HELEN. Crystal. Through and through.
NATALIE. What are you asking?
HELEN. I'm sorry, it's sold.
NATALIE. But what if I love it?
HELEN. Even if you don't love it, it went this morning.
ESTELLE. Natalie, come here.

(NATALIE *joins* ESTELLE *as a car horn is heard Offstage.*)

HELEN. (*Looks in its direction, calls out.*) Bea!

(*She collects her coat and bag.* BEA *enters from the back.*)

BEA. Yes, Helen?
HELEN. I gotta go. It's Jack. I'll be back as soon as he's finished.

(*The horn sounds again.*)

BEA. Tell him good luck for me.
HELEN. It's just a physical. He'll live to be a hundred. I'll see you later. (*She exits.*)
BEA. (*To* NATALIE *and* ESTELLE.) Can I help you?
ESTELLE. We're just looking.
NATALIE. We love to go junking. (*Holding up headdress.*) How much are you asking for this?
BEA. (*Smiles.*) Oh that. I bought that for my son in—uh—1954 from a real Indian in New Mexico. Have you ever been to New Mexico?
NATALIE. No.

7

BEA. These are very hard to find. It's genuine Hopi but you can have it for $6.95.

NATALIE. Hmm . . .

(ANGIE—*a coat over her waitress uniform—enters with* MARTHA.)

ANGIE. Lunch!

BEA. (*Taking paper bag from her.*) Thanks, oh, Angie, you're a doll.

ANGIE. It's a dollar eighty. Just put it against what I owe you. This is my friend, Martha Feeny. Martha, say hello to Bea Asher.

BEA. Hello.

MARTHA. Hello. Angie said you had a fabulous boa.

ANGIE. The lavender one, you know?

BEA. Oh yes. (*She crosses to racks, sees* NATALIE *and* ESTELLE *exiting.*) Did you find anything else?

ESTELLE. We're not sure.

NATALIE. We'll be back.

BEA. What about the headdress? Don't you want it?

NATALIE. I don't think so. I like it very much except for the feathers.

BEA. (*To* MARTHA.) Here you are.

(NATALIE *and* ESTELLE *exit.* BEA *offers the boa.*)

MARTHA. Oh, it's a stunner! (*She puts it around her neck, then on the back of her arms.*)

ANGIE. It's fab, honey. And you got just the elbows for it.

MARTHA. God, it must be a fortune.

BEA. It's eight dollars, marked down from ten thousand.

MARTHA. I'll take it! Oh, it's gorgeous! (*Getting money from purse.*) It'll kill 'em at the Stardust, won't it, Angie?

ANGIE. It's a knockout, babe.

(MARTHA *hands* BEA *money.*)

BEA. Let me wrap it for you.

MARTHA. Do you mind?

BEA. (*Taking boa.*) No trouble. I've got plenty of gift newspaper around here. (*As* BEA *wraps boa.*)

MARTHA. (*To* ANGIE.) Don't you love it?

ANGIE. It's a terrific buy. And you'll be right on time for the beauty parlor.

MARTHA. It's just one block down, right?

ANGIE. Out the door, hang a left. It's on the same side of the street. And be sure to ask for Beverly. She does things your hair won't believe.

BEA. (*Hands* MARTHA *her package.*) Here you are.

MARTHA. Thanks, hon.

BEA. Thank you.

MARTHA. See you tonight?

ANGIE. You better believe it.

MARTHA. (*To* BEA.) Goodbye.

BEA. Goodbye. It was nice meeting you.

MARTHA. It really was. Bye again. (*She exits.*)

BEA. She seems very nice.

ANGIE. What about you, Bea? (BEA *doesn't understand the question.*) What've you got on for tonight? You going to have dinner with Walter Cronkite again, then hit the sack with Johnny Carson?

BEA. (*Wearily.*) Angie . . .

ANGIE. Look, you can tell me to mind my own business.

BEA. (*Good naturedly.*) When did that ever stop you?

ANGIE. It's just I know where you're coming from. It took me six months after *my* husband died to realize they only buried one of us. How long's it been for you now? A year?

BEA. Just about. A little more.

ANGIE. So?

BEA. So what?

ANGIE. So when are you going to start having some fun, giving yourself some pleasure?

BEA. (*Defensively.*) Who says I don't?

ANGIE. Waiting for a call from your son once a week? Sitting for your daughter 'cause for the kids it's a treat and for her it's free?

BEA. Angie, that's not fair.

ANGIE. You want fair or honest? You're wasting yourself, babe. I'm watching you start to fade right into the woodwork. (*Beat . . .*) Bea, come to the Stardust. There's a terrific band and a real nice crowd. Come tonight.

BEA. Oh, Angie, please. Grandmothers don't go dancing.

ANGIE. Who said? The Stardust is full of 'em. We got people

there with one foot in the grave and the other doin' the Mambo. How old do you think *I* am, for Chriss-sake?

BEA. I don't know. Forty seven, forty eight?

ANGIE. (*Proudly.*) And what's the matter with fifty-four?

BEA. You're not!

ANGIE. Who lies about something like that? You think Martha before's some kind of chicken? That lady's got five grown up kids.

BEA. Five kids! God, she doesn't look it.

ANGIE. I'm telling you, there's no one at the Stardust doesn't have a lot of mileage, but you'll never have a better time. (*Evenly.*) Make your move, kid. A year's more'n enough. The years have a way of becoming forever, y'know. (*As* BEA *reflects on this,* ANGIE *checks her watch.*) I gotta cut. I'm gonna have lunch somewhere, then get back to the diner.

BEA. Angie, I'll see you tomorrow.

ANGIE. Do yourself a favor. See me tonight. The Stardust Ballroom. Bea, you name it; Rhumba, Samba, Hustle, Waltz, Lindy—God! The Lindy! If you do come by, just look for a long pair of legs stickin' way up in the air—My face'll be right under 'em! (*She exits.* BEA *watches her go.*)

OUTSIDE THE BALLROOM

COUPLES *are arriving.*

MARIO. (*To* ANITRA.) Hiya, gorgeous. (*He kisses* ANITRA'S *cheeks, as* KARL *kisses* EMILY'S.)

KARL. Emily.

ANITRA. Hello, Mario. (*As* EMILY *and* MARIO *move on.*)

MARIO. I don't believe it. She keeps getting prettier.

EMILY. What else has she got to do?

(HARRY *entering with* MARIE.)

HARRY. Mario!

EMILY. (*Overlapping.*) Hi, Marie.

MARIE. Emily. (EMILY *and* MARIE *press cheeks, kiss the air.*)

HARRY. (*To* MARIO.) Here's that five from last week. You're a sweetheart.

MARIO. (*Taking the bill.*) There's no big hurry, you know, if you need it.

HARRY. It's okay, I'm alright now. My son raised my allowance.

MARIO. (*Smiles.*) Beautiful.

(MARTHA *and* PETEY *enter.*)

MARIE. Martha! (*Nodding at beige boa.*) Martha, that boa is *fan*-tastic!

MARTHA. (*Modeling it.*) You like?

MARIE. Gorgeous!

PETEY. It oughta be, for a hundred bucks. (*Calls.*) Hey, Mario. I didn't forget. (*Handing* MARIO *folded paper.*) Here's the Scarsdale Diet. It really works.

EMILY. (*Taking paper from* MARIO.) Oh, you're not fat—and I love every ton of you.

MARIE. Shirley!

EMILY. (*Spotting the entrance of* SHIRLEY *and* PAUL.) Shirley! Welcome back!

MARTHA. God, you gave us all a scare.

SHIRLEY. I couldn't be better, honest. The doctor said it wasn't my heart, it was just my nerves.

MARIE. Your nerves?

EMILY. Oh, there's so much of that now.

THOMAS. (*Entering.*) Shirley!

SHIRLEY. Thomas. (*Hugging* MARGARET *at his side.*) Margaret.

MARGARET. You look beautiful, my darling.

SHIRLEY. And here's the reason. Everybody, this is Paul. We met in the hospital. He took my X-rays.

MARIO. And then something developed, right?

(ALL *laugh.*)

PAUL. Come on, dear. Let's dance.

SHIRLEY. Yes, Paul, let's never stop. (*They exit.* BEA *enters.*)

THERE'S A TERRIFIC BAND AND A REAL NICE CROWD

BEA.
"THERE'S A TERRIFIC BAND AND A REAL NICE
    CROWD,"
THAT'S WHAT ANGIE SAID.

NEVER WILL UNDERSTAND, WITH A WHOLE EVENING
   PLANNED
HOW I GOT HERE INSTEAD!

I DEFROSTED A LAMB CHOP AND WAS GOING TO
   WATCH
A MOVIE ON TV
NOW I'M STANDING UNDER A NEON SIGN
WATCHING IT SHINE ON ME!

"THERE'S A TERRIFIC BAND AND A REAL NICE
   CROWD"
AND IT'LL DO ME GOOD TO GET OUT.
IT ISN'T A SINGLES BAR—IT'S ONLY A BALLROOM!
SO WHAT AM I SO NERVOUS ABOUT?

WHAT IF NO ONE ASKS ME TO DANCE?
WHAT IF SOMEONE ASKS ME TO DANCE?
WHAT IF I CATCH THE NEXT BUS?

BUT ANGIE SAYS THERE'S A REAL NICE CROWD
AND THAT BAND SURE KNOWS HOW TO PLAY!
I'LL JUST GO IN AND SEE WHAT IT'S LIKE
I DON'T HAVE TO STAY.

MAYBE IT WOULDN'T BE SO BAD—
IF I HAD SOMEONE TO WALK IN WITH.
MAURY, IF YOU WERE HERE . . .
BUT THEN, MAURY, IF YOU WERE HERE,
I WOULDN'T BE HERE TO BEGIN WITH!

IS IT A CLUB FOR BOOZERS,
A HAVEN FOR LOSERS
WHO COME TO ESCAPE THE TRUTH?
ONE OF THOSE PLACES
WITH PAINTED PARTY FACES
FULL OF MIDDLE-AGED PEOPLE RELIVING THEIR
   YOUTH?
MAYBE IT'S MORE LIKE A PARTY—
WITH COLORED LIGHTS CIRCLING THE FLOOR,
WHERE EVERYTHING'S PRETTY AND YOU DANCE AND
   DREAM

AND YOU CHECK YOUR COAT AND CARES AT THE
   DOOR.

"THERE'S A TERRIFIC BAND AND A REAL NICE
   CROWD"
THAT'S WHAT ANGIE SAID.
PART OF ME SAYS: "GO HOME",
BUT THERE'S ANOTHER PART SAYING "GO AHEAD"
SINCE THEY'RE BOTH SAYING "MAKE YOUR MIND
   UP!"
WHADDAYA THINK, TWINKLE TOES?
A LITTLE MORE LIPSTICK—AND MAYBE SOME
   ROUGE—
HERE GOES!
WHAT HAVE YOU GOT TO LOSE?
ONLY A NIGHT—WHO CARES
IT ISN'T THE MATTERHORN
IT'S ONLY A FLIGHT OF STAIRS.
WHY DON'T YOU TRY IT?
YOU MIGHT EVEN LIKE IT? . . .
WHO KNOWS?
   (BEA *exits*.)

THE BALLROOM

COUPLES *dancing*. OTHERS *are arriving*.

SONG FOR DANCING

  MARLENE.
PLAY A SONG FOR DANCIN'
ALL NIGHT LONG FOR DANCIN'
FOX-TROT, BOSSA NOVA
WATCH MY FEET TAKE 'OVAH'
PLAY FOR ME FOR DANCIN'
ONE, TWO, THREE, FOR DANCIN'
WHILE I SLIDE AND SLIP IN
FANCY STEPS LIKE DIPPIN'

WHEN THE HIPS ARE MOVIN'
THINGS BEGIN IMPROVIN'

WITH THE LIMBS IN ACTION
INSTANT SATISFACTION
THAT'S THE MENU—WHEN YOU KNOW HOW.
SO, FOR ME THE ANSWER
IS TO BE A DANCER,
WHEN THE BEAT'S INSPIRED
FEET CANNOT GET TIRED.
MAKE IT STRONG FOR DANCIN'
ALL NIGHT LONG FOR DANCIN'
PLAY A SONG FOR DANCIN' NOW!
   NATHAN.
KINDLY UNDERSCORE US
THROUGH ANOTHER CHORUS,
VIENNESE OR LATIN,
KEEP IT SMOOTH AS SATIN.
SLOW STEP, SLOW THEN QUICK BEAT,
DRUMMER HIT THAT KICK BEAT,
WHEN I HEAR THOSE SAXES
EV'RYTHING RELAXES.

IF I HOLD HER TIGHTLY,
EASE THE TEMPO SLIGHTLY,
AS I WHISPER TO HER
LET THE LYRIC WOO HER.
   NATHAN and MARLENE.
DANCIN' HELPS ROMANCIN' YOU'LL SEE
DANCIN' ON A DIME STEP,
EV'RY TAKE YOUR TIME STEP,
ARM IN ARM WE'RE WALKIN'
BODIES DO THE TALKIN'
MAKE IT STRONG FOR DANCIN'
ALL NIGHT LONG FOR DANCIN'
PLAY A SONG . . .
FOR DANCIN' FOR ME

        (*A tentative* BEA *enters, looks around.*)

   BILL. (*In passing.*) Can I help you?
   BEA. I'm looking for a friend.
   BILL. That's the name of the game.
   BEA. Would you know if Angie's around?

BILL. We got two Angies come in here. One's about five foot nothin', the other's a tall blonde, legs up to her ears.

BEA. That's the one.

ANGIE. (*Behind them, calls.*) Bea!

BILL. (*Without turning.*) She's here. (*He goes as a delighted* ANGIE *joins* BEA.)

BEA. Angie!

ANGIE. Bea, God bless ya, you decided to come.

BEA. (*Uncertainly.*) Just 'cause I'm here doesn't mean I decided.

ANGIE. (*Helpfully.*) Relax, babe.

BEA. I haven't felt like this in years. Like I'm at a prom.

ANGIE. Every night's a prom here. Who says we're entitled to have only one.

BEA. But, everybody's so gussied up. Look at me.

ANGIE. You look fine.

BEA. Fine is nothing here.

ANGIE. That's the Stardust. This crowd is really into clothes. They spend every penny on dressing up, then go home and have a can of dog food. (BEA *laughs.*) Good girl. Enjoy. Let's have a drink. I'm buyin'. Bill! (*To* BEA.) What do you like?

BEA. I don't want anything. Oh, I don't know. (*She shrugs.*) What do people drink?

ANGIE. Jesus, where you been, in a mineshaft?

BILL. (*To* ANGIE.) Did you get the message from Lightfeet?

BILL and ANGIE. (*In unison.*) He's gonna be a little late.

ANGIE. Why doesn't he just tatoo that on your forehead?

BILL. What'll ya have? Your usual?

ANGIE. Make it two.

(BILL *goes.*)

BEA. Wait! What am I having.

ANGIE. You'll love it. A Danish Bloody Bull. It's consomme, tomato juice, aquavidt and a stick of celery.

BEA. That's more than I had for dinner.

ANGIE. Really loosens you up for dancin'. You'll see.

(MARTHA *and* PETEY *dance up.*)

MARTHA. Hi, Angie. Hi, Bea.

BEA. Hi!

MARTHA. Martha, remember?

BEA. Yes, I remember. Hi.

MARTHA. The boa is a smash.

ANGIE. I told you.

MARTHA. Petey, this is Angie's friend, Bea.

PETEY. Hello, Angie's friend, Bea.

BEA. Hello.

PETEY. (*To* MARTHA.) Okay, babe?

MARTHA. (*To* ANGIE *and* BEA.) We gotta dance. Petey doesn't dance for five minutes, he gets the bends.

BEA. (*Speaks appreciatively.*) Five kids—with a figure like that.

ANGIE. She never eats. Petey's in appliances. If you ever need a refrigerator or anything like that, he'll give it to you for cost. Just don't get trapped in the stockroom. (SCOOTER *comes up behind them. He pinches* ANGIE.) Bea, this is Scooter—the claw machine.

SCOOTER. Am I gonna get to dance with you, ANGIE?

ANGIE. If Lightfeet doesn't make it.

SCOOTER. Tell your friend, am I lyin'? (*To* BEA.) I'd buy this woman anything she wants; cars, jewelry, furs. Everything I have is hers, if she'd only look my way. Once! (*He goes.*)

BEA. God, Angie, he's crazy about you.

ANGIE. (*Nods.*) Yeah, he went bankrupt two months ago. But he's okay. He's good people.

(*As* MARGARET *and* THOMAS *dance by:*)

THOMAS. Hi, Angie!

ANGIE. Hi, Thomas! Hi, Margaret!

MARGARET. Hello!

ANGIE. Margaret, that dress is outta sight.

MARGARET. Thank you, Angie.

ANGIE. This is my friend, Bea.

THOMAS. Hi.

MARGARET. Hello! (*They dance Off.*)

BEA. She's beautiful.

ANGIE. Uh huh. *And* she's a grandma.

BEA. Really? (ANGIE *nods.*) Has anyone told her?

(*Drumroll.*)

NATHAN BRICKER. Ladies and gentlemen, your very kind attention, please. A few announcements from the Queen of the Stardust Ballroom, Pauline Krim.

(*Applause.*)

PAULINE. Thank you. First, let me tell you about some wonderful coming events in the future days ahead here at the Stardust. Next month's contest is going to be the Tango. So brush up on your steps and I want to see all you Valentinos sign up at the bar. Secondly, Fay Halpern, our very dedicated Hustle teacher, has a message now with great importance for us all. Fay.

FAY. Thank you, Pauline. I really want to talk to the men tonight.

SCOOTER. Talk to me, talk to me.

(*Scattered laughter.*)

FAY. Please. The third hustle lesson is this Saturday afternoon. So far, we've had a lot of women joining up but not nearly enough men. Now, if we're really serious about the hustle, you guys are going to have to start pulling your share, right?

VARIOUS MEN. Right. Okay. For sure, Fay, etc. . . .

FAY. Thank you.

PAULINE. Also, the management has asked me to inform you that 20% discounts are available to all Stardust regulars at Brandt's Shoe Store on Fordham Road. So don't be afraid to wear out your shoe leather! Remember Brandt Shoe Store's Famous Slogan— (*Consulting her notes.*) "Put Your Feet in Our Hands." (*Continuing.*) Well, that about winds me up. Unless there's anything else . . .

MR. FRIENDLY. I'd like to drink to Shirley Selwin's health! It's good to have you back, Shirley.

VARIOUS VOICES. Yeah, Shirley. Welcome back, Shirley . . .

ANGIE. (*Realizing.*) Shirley! (*She rushes to* SHIRLEY *for a hug.*)

SHIRLEY. Angie! (*A speech.*) Angie . . . Everybody . . . How can I thank you for your wonderful cards and all your calls? Laying on my back at the hospital, all I could see looking up—at the ceiling— (*Looking up.*) was the Stardust ball. (*To* CROWD.) It's so great to be back home..

(*Applause.*)

PAULINE. Okay, boys and girls, let's dance.

(JOHNNY LIGHTFEET *enters*.)

SHIRLEY. Lightfeet!

LIGHTFEET. Shirley! Lookin' good!

ANGIE. Lightfeet!

LIGHTFEET. Hiya, doll. (*He kisses* ANGIE.)

ANGIE. What happened?

LIGHTFEET. Ah, my wife started in on me again. God, sometimes she acts like we're married.

ANGIE. I'd like you to meet my friend, Bea.

LIGHTFEET. Pleased to meet you, Bea.

BEA. How do you do?

LIGHTFEET. (*To* ANGIE.) Come on. Let's dance.

ANGIE. I'm with somebody, Johnny.

LIGHTFEET. What are ya talking about?

BEA. Angie, please go ahead.

ANGIE. Johnny'll get you a partner.

BEA. Angie, you don't have to worry about me. Angie!

ANGIE. (*Taking* JOHNNY *aside*.) Look, Bea's the one I been tellin' you about come's into the diner. She's been havin' a rough time. Her husband's in the ground, her son moved to California and her daughter's a pain in the ass. So it's time for a little do-unto-others, okay? Get her somebody to dance with.

LIGHTFEET. No sweat. (*Crossing*.) Lemme just see how tall you are.

BEA. This really isn't necessary . . .

LIGHTFEET. (*Finishing sizing her up*.) Be back in a sec. (*He goes*.)

BEA. (*Terribly uncomfortable*.) Angie, I'm spoiling your time—and his.

ANGIE. Look, you're with me. That means I'm with you.

BEA. Well, the samba really isn't my dance anyway.

ANGIE. Oh, great. Johnny got you "The Noodle."

BEA. The Noodle?

ANGIE. "Harry-something-or-other." I remember his name, I just forget it. He's a terrific dancer for his age.

LIGHTFEET. Harry, this is Bea.

HARRY. Enchanted. (*He kisses* BEA'S *hand*.) Shall we? (*He escorts* BEA *onto the floor*.)

LIGHTFEET. Can we dance now?

ANGIE. Just lemme make sure she's alright.

(BEA *and* HARRY *dance.*)

BEA. I think I've had enough!

HARRY. What?

BEA. You're wonderful. You're really wonderful! Look at you! You're too good for me.

HARRY. Please don't stop. I'm too good for everybody. (*He follows* BEA *back to* ANGIE, *leaves her with a bow.*) Charmed.

BEA. I'll see ya tomorrow, Angie.

ANGIE. Hey, hey, hey. Where you runnin'? What's wrong?

BEA. Everything, everything. Starting with me. I don't belong here, Angie.

ANGIE. Look, it took me six months to get you out. I'm not going to let you turn around and crawl back into your shell.

BEA. Angie, I'm not ready for this. All these people, they're so . . . oh, I don't know. They're so . . .

ANGIE. Alive, that's the word you're looking for. Alive. And so are you, Bea. You're alive and you're a woman.

BEA. No! Not like these. They're so graceful, so beautiful.

ANGIE. It's the place. You'll learn. It's the make-up and the light. It's Shangri-La. The minute half these women walk out the front door, their faces fall off.

(*Drumroll.*)

NATHAN. Will the owner of a red Pontiac, license plate XY0769 like to wave goodbye to it as it's being towed away?

EMILY. Oh, no, not again!

(*She runs Off to laughter and jibes.* PAULINE *crosses to* BEA.)

PAULINE. (*To* BEA.) Hi.

BEA. Hello.

PAULINE. Firsttimer?

BEA. Yes.

PAULINE. (*Offering her hand.*) Pauline Krim.

BEA. Bea Asher.

PAULINE. Asher. Any relation to Dr. Asher? Nate and Vi?

BEA. No, no relation.

PAULINE. Oh. Well, I know quite a few Ashers.

BEA. My husband's name was Maurice.

(AL ROSSI *enters the ballroom and starts to walk across the floor.*)

MARIO. Hi, Al. Waddayah say?
AL. Oh, hi, Mario. (*Spotting* PAULINE.) Hi, Pauline.
PAULINE. Hi, Al. Al, come over here, meet a firsttimer. Al Rossi, Bea Asher.
BEA and AL. (*Together.*) How do you do?
AL. Firsttimer?
BEA. Very much so.
AL. Would you care to dance?
BEA. (*Uncomfortably.*) Not right now. I'm—I'm just sort of—
AL. (*Helpfully.*) Getting the feel of the place.
BEA. Yeah, it takes a while.
AL. I know, tell me about it.

(BILL *appears with* BEA'S *drink. It is bright red, in a very large glass, celery stick and all.*)

BILL. Here's your drink.
AL. Well, that should help you get the feel pretty fast.

(BILL *goes Off.*)

BEA. (*Looking at drink.*) A friend ordered it. I really can't drink it.
AL. Would you like me to take it away?
BEA. Would you mind? You could give it to a poor family. (*They both smile.*)
AL. Look, how about later? Do you think maybe we could dance later?
BEA. Well, let's see, alright?
AL. Of course. Thank you.

(*He goes Off. Lindy vamp begins.*)

LIGHTFEET. (*To* ANGIE.) What do ya' say, sweetheart, can we dance now? It's a Lindy.
ANGIE. (*To* BEA.) You mind? You won't disappear?

BEA. Angie, if you don't cut it out and dance I *will* leave!
ANGIE. Great! 'Cause I can never say no to a Lindy.

(LIGHTFEET *leads here to the dance floor where they have their
chance to do what they do best—a Lindy.*)

ONE BY ONE

NATHAN and MARLENE.
ONE BY ONE
THEY'RE GOIN' TWO BY TWO—
JUST WATCH 'EM
ONE BY ONE
THEY KNOW WHAT NOAH KNEW.
HE KNOW IT'S NOT MUCH FUN
UNLESS IT'S HE AND SHE AND YOU AND ME!

(*Dance Chorus.*)

NATHAN.
ONE BY ONE—
MARLENE.
BABY, WHAT ARE YOU DOIN' TONIGHT?
NATHAN.
ONE BY ONE—
MARLENE.
HOW ABOUT US TWO BY TWOIN' IT TONIGHT?
NATHAN.
TWO BY TWO—
MARLENE.
THERE'S JUST NO SENSE IN GIVIN' IT UP.
NATHAN.
ME AND YOU—
MARLENE.
NOT WHEN WE COULD BE LIVIN' IT UP.
NATHAN and MARLENE.
WE'VE GOT TIME AND NOTHIN' TO LOSE
BY PROVIN' THINGS ARE BETTER BY TWOS!
(*Dance Chorus*)
ONE IS GOOD FOR SOLITAIRE
AND THREE'S A CROWD NO MATTER WHERE.
FOUR'S FOR DOUBLES ON THE TENNIS COURT

AND FIVES A POPULAR INDOOR SPORT.
IT ALL DEPENDS ON WHAT YOU WANNA DO
FOR WHAT WE'VE GOT IN MIND, THE NUMBER IS
TWO!

(*By the time the dance ends* AL *is beside* BEA.)

NATHAN. Very good dancers . . .
AL. (*To* BEA.) Hi. Al Rossi.
BEA. I remember.
AL. You said maybe later. Is this later enough?
BEA. (*Smiles.*) I guess so.
NATHAN. Okay all you Latin lovers, let's try a Cha-Cha-Cha!

(AL *takes her gently by the arm and leads her to the floor.* AL *is a fine and considerate leader.* BEA *is a little stiff, but* AL *is so confident and graceful and easy to follow that very soon something wonderful begins to happen to* BEA. *She follows* AL *around the dance floor—free, inspired. Then, a Montage of* BEA *and* AL *dancing the Chacha, Merengue, the Rhumba, and finally . . .*)

NATHAN. And, now, for your listening pleasure, here's the lovely Marlene.

(MARLENE *steps to the microphone and sings as* BEA *and* AL *and* SOME *of the* OTHER DANCERS *dance the Fox-trot.*)

DREAMS

MARLENE.
DREAMS—QUIETLY SPINNING,
DREAMS—SONGS WITHOUT WORDS
A WORLD OF WISHES AND MEM'RIES,
LOST IN TIME—
FOUND IN DREAMS—
WHERE NOTHING'S FORGOTTEN—
NOT A MOMENT YOU'VE EVER KNOWN.
THEY SLEEP BY DAY—
THEY DANCE BY NIGHT—
THEIR ARMS ARE NEVER FAR.
TRUST YOUR DREAMS,

JUST YOUR DREAMS,
FOR THEY KNOW WHO YOU ARE.

(*Music ends.*)

AL. How are you doing?

BEA. I don't know. You tell me.

AL. You're doing great.

BEA. You make it easy. You could be a pro.

AL. Can you imagine, being paid to dance? It's a little bit different from what I do.

BEA. Oh?

AL. I'm with the government.

BEA. (*A bit more interested.*) Oh?

AL. I'm a mailman.

BEA. Really? A mailman?

AL. That's right. I'm a man of letters.

BEA. Well, I never would have guessed.

AL. Would you have danced with me if you had?

BEA. Of course. What does it matter what people do?

AL. I always say that.

BEA. You do?

AL. Yes.

BEA. (*In that case . . .*) I run a Junk Store.

AL. A Junk Store?

BEA. See, when my husband died, I couldn't get a job and I had all these clothes, and stuff around the house, so I opened up a Junk Store. I'm selling this dress tomorrow.

AL. I think you look very nice.

BEA. I know I don't, but I'm feeling nicer all the time. I haven't danced like this in years and years.

AL. Really?

BEA. Really. My husband lost interest after the children were born.

AL. Oh?

BEA. In dancing.

AL. Oh. Well, the way you've been dancing tonight, it seems like you've been dancing every day of your life.

BEA. (*Touched.*) Thank you.

(AL *pulls her closer. She coughs.*)

MARLENE.
THEY SLEEP BY DAY
THEY DANCE BY NIGHT—
THEIR ARMS ARE NEVER FAR.
TRUST YOUR DREAMS,
JUST YOUR DREAMS,
FOR THEY KNOW WHO YOU ARE.

ANGIE. (*Appearing.*) Bea, Martha and I are splitting a cab.
AL. (*Meaning* BEA.) Oh, she'll be alright.
ANGIE. (*To* BEA.) You want us to drop you?
AL. (*To* BEA.) I'll take you home.
BEA. Oh, no. I'm going with the girls.
AL. It would be my pleasure.
BEA. I don't want to take you out of your way.
AL. Well, maybe it's not, and who cares if it is?
BEA. You probably have to get up early in the morning.
ANGIE. Not as early as me. What do ya' say, Bea?
BEA. I'm coming with you, Angie.
ANGIE. Good night, Al.
AL. Good night, Angie.
BEA. Good night and thank you. (*She starts to leave.*)
AL. Oh, Bea?
BEA. (*Stops.*) Yes?
AL. I'd like to call you.
BEA. Oh,—I don't think so.
AL. For dinner, maybe? Take in a show?
BEA. No, really I don't think so.
AL. Are you coming back to the Stardust?
BEA. Well, I don't know. I don't know what my plans are.
AL. Well try, huh? I'll be watching for you. Al Rossi?
BEA. I remember.
AL. Good night.
BEA. Good night. Thank you. (AL *leaves.*)
ANGIE. Well, somebody did alright for herself tonight, huh?

SOMEBODY DID ALRIGHT

BEA.
SOMEBODY DID ALRIGHT FOR HERSELF TONIGHT—
    CHA, CHA, CHA!

SOMEBODY HAD QUITE A NIGHT FOR HERSELF
    TONIGHT—CHA, CHA, CHA!
SOMEBODY SURE SURPRISED HERSELF,
HARDLY RECOGNIZED HERSELF,
SOMEONE FORGOT HERSELF,
SOMEONE WAS NOT HERSELF.
    MARLENE'S VOICE.
DREAMS—QUIETLY SPINNING,
DREAMS—SONGS WITHOUT . . .
    BEA.
SOMEONE'S ALIVE AND KICKIN' AGAIN TONIGHT—
    CHA, CHA, CHA!
SOMEBODY FELT LIKE A CHICKEN AGAIN TONIGHT—
    CHA, CHA, CHA!
FORGOT SHE WAS WEARING SHOES TONIGHT,
EVEN MISSED THE NEWS TONIGHT.
MUSIC STILL HAS ITS CHARMS,
WHEN YOU'RE IN SOMEONE'S ARMS,
    MARLENE'S VOICE.
A WORLD OF WISHES AND MEM'RIES
LOST IN TIME—
FOUND IN . . .
    BEA.
SOMEBODY SHOULD HAVE STAYED AT THE STORE
    TONIGHT—CHA, CHA, CHA!
WHO KNOWS WHAT SHE COULD HAVE MADE AT THE
    STORE TONIGHT—CHA, CHA, CHA!
SOMEONE WHO CAN'T WAIT TO WORK,
TOMORROW MAY BE LATE TO WORK.
SOMEBODY TOOK A CHANCE—
SOMEBODY STILL CAN DANCE.

BEA'S LIVING ROOM

HELEN. (*Enters.*) Bea, for God's sake, where have you been?
BEA. Helen, it's one o'clock!
HELEN. Oh, I know. I know it's one o'clock a lot better than
you do.
BEA. What's wrong? Is it one of the children? One of the
girls?
HELEN. They're fine, everyone's fine. It's you.
BEA. Me?

HELEN. (*Interrupting.*) I have been calling you all night. I called here, I called the store, I called Diane. My God. I'd better call her. (*As she dials.*) We were sure you were lying in some alleyway with your head split open. It's not just strangers in the newspapers, you know. If Jack didn't stop me, I would have called the police.

BEA. Where is Jack?

HELEN. Looking for a place to park. The man is a saint. He drove me in his pajamas. (*Into phone.*) Diane? Aunt Helen. Your mother's home. She just walked in. She's fine. (*Listens.*) I didn't ask her. (*To* BEA.) Where were you?

BEA. I went dancing.

HELEN. Dancing?

BEA. At the Stardust Ballroom.

HELEN. Dancing? (*Into phone.*) Yes that's what she said, I—

BEA. Let me talk to her. (*She takes the phone.*) Diane? Honey, I'm sorry if you were worried. No, I'm alright. I was just out with some friends . . . yes, honey, I know it's late, so why don't you go to bed and get some sleep? And I'll call you tomorrow. I'm alright. Yes! Good night, sweetheart. (*She hangs up, pleased.*) She was worried.

HELEN. We were all worried. Who would have suspected you were having a good time?

BEA. It's easier to think of me dead then dancing, isn't it, Helen?

(*A weary* JACK *enters, a raincoat over his pajamas, street shoes and a hat.*)

JACK. I must be ten blocks from here.

HELEN. She's home.

JACK. You alright, Bea?

BEA. I'm fine, Jack.

HELEN. You know where she was? Dancing!

JACK. Honest to God? Dancing? A whole evening?

BEA. Uh huh. I love to dance. I'd forgotten.

JACK. That's terrific. Alright, Helen. She's alive. Let's go.

HELEN. Who'd you dance with?

JACK. I gotta be at the doctor at eight.

HELEN. Bea?

BEA. There was someone there. A very nice man.

HELEN. You met him at the ballroom?

BEA. Yes.

HELEN. Who is he? What does he do?

BEA. He's a mailman.

HELEN. A mailman? You danced with a mailman? (*To* JACK.) She danced with a mailman.

JACK. You'd think at night they'd want to sit down.

BEA. Helen, he's a terrific dancer.

JACK. (*Impatiently.*) Helen.

HELEN. (*Annoyed.*) Jack, don't "Helen" me. (*To* BEA.) You intend to see him again, he's so terrific?

BEA. I don't know. I told you Helen. I met a nice man. And we danced. I enjoyed myself. I'd forgotten how to do that, too.

HELEN. Just remember your family, Bea. Your family cares about you. More than outsiders. More than any strange mailmen. Blood is thicker, Bea. I don't have to tell you.

JACK. Helen, I gotta take a stress test in the morning!

HELEN. So you gotta give me one tonight? (*Kissing* BEA.) It's out of love, Bea.

BEA. I know, Helen. Good night. Good night, Jack.

JACK. Good night, dancer.

(HELEN *and* JACK *exit. The phone rings.*)

BEA. (*Running to answer the phone.*) Hello? (*Surprised.*) How did you get my number? (*Listens, remembers.*) Oh, yes, I guess I did mention his name to Pauline. You're a very good detective . . . (*Listens, then.*) Oh, I don't know. I don't know if I can dance two nights in a row. (*Listens, then.*) Well, of course you can, but not here. Why don't you call me at work. Have you got a pencil? Ludlow 3-4789. Don't lose it. (*Straight.*) It's an unlisted junk store. (*Pause.*) Al . . . thank you for calling. Good night. (*She hangs up. She sings.*)

THERE'S A TERRIFIC BAND AND A REAL NICE
    CROWD—
JUST LIKE ANGIE SAID.
I HAD A TERRIFIC TIME
SINCE WHEN IS IT SUCH A CRIME
TO BE LATE FOR BED?

IT WAS JUST LIKE A PARTY WITH COLORED LIGHTS
    CIRCLING THE FLOOR

WHERE EVERYTHING'S PRETTY AND I DANCED AND ...
> MARLENE'S VOICE.

... DREAMS—
WHERE NOTHING'S FORGOTTEN—
NOT A MOMENT
YOU'VE EVER KNOWN.
> BEA and MARLENE'S VOICE.

THEY SLEEP BY DAY—
THEN DANCE AT NIGHT—
THEIR ARMS ARE NEVER FAR.
> MARLENE'S VOICE.

TRUST YOUR DREAMS.
> BEA.

TRUST YOUR DREAMS,
> MARLENE'S VOICE.

JUST YOUR DREAMS,
> BEA.

JUST YOUR DREAMS,
> BEA and MARLENE'S VOICE.

FOR THEY KNOW WHO YOU ...
> BEA.

SOMEBODY HAD QUITE A NIGHT FOR HERSELF—
DID ALRIGHT FOR HERSELF—
TONIGHT—CHA, CHA, CHA!

THE BALLROOM

NATHAN. Ladies and Gentlemen, the moment has come. It's your Tango Contest! Presenting our first contestants—Emily and Mario! (*Applause. Tango Music. The contest begins. EMILY and MARIO dance on, over start of music.*) Emily and her Mario—just in this country one year and already he dances like a native. (EMILY *and* MARIO *finish.*) Very good, kids! And now our second couple! Bea and Al! (BEA *and* AL *dance on.*) Aren't they wonderful? They've been dancing together for only one month, and already they're joined at the hip! (*At finish of* BEA *and* AL:) Now let's welcome Martha and Petey! (MARTHA *and* PETEY *dance on.*) There they are—Beauty and the Beard! (*After* MARTHA *and* PETEY.) Anitra and Karl! (ANITRA *and* KARL *dance on.*) The lovebirds of the Stardust Ballroom—every step a caress! (*After* ANITRA *and* KARL.) Shirley and Paul! (SHIRLEY *and* PAUL *dance on.*) And we thought she'd never dance again! (*After*

SHIRLEY *and* PAUL.) Margaret and Thomas! (MARGARET *and* THOMAS *dance on.*) Class with a capital "K." (*After* MARGARET *and* THOMAS.) Marie and Harry! (MARIE *and* HARRY *dance on.*) Yes, sir. It's sunny Spain right here in the Bronx. (*After* MARIE *and* HARRY.) And now, let's have one more look at all our wonderful couples!

(ALL COUPLES dance, then take their bows.)

PAULINE. Weren't they something? I just wish they could all win. Tonight's judges are as follows . . . (*Consulting notes.*) Judging skill and originality, one of your youngest couples, Christina and Russ. Judging style, Mr. Lester Mulvahill, who won the Tango Cup two years running, or should I say dancing? Judging appearance, a woman whose own appearance leaves everything about her to be desired—Eleanor Martin. And it falls on me to judge the last category—feeling. Give us one moment to tally the votes, please. (*The* JUDGES *confer.*)

BEA. I think it's Marie and the Noodle.

AL. Nah, we got it cold.

LIGHTFEET. You alright, Shirley?

SHIRLEY. (*Hyperventilating.*) It's just my nerves.

ANGIE. Jesus, they're getting loud.

SHIRLEY. (*Still hyperventilating.*) This is just what happened when they thought I was having a heart attack. I'll be fine. I'll just sit here and be quiet.

PAULINE. Attention, people! We have our winners! (*Drumroll.*) Second prize goes to—Anitra and Karl!

ANITRA. Second!

(*Applause as* ANITRA *and* KARL *accept the Bronze Trophy.*)

PAULINE. And now, first prize . . . (*Drumroll.*) This beautiful silver trophy goes to . . . Shirley and Paul!

(*A scream from* SHIRLEY, *as she runs to* PAULINE *with* PAUL *to accept their trophy.*)

BEA. Speech. Speech, Shirley. (OTHERS *pick up the suggestion.*)

SHIRLEY. (*To* ALL.) Oh, God. What can I say? I guess next to finding out I was going to live, this is the happiest moment of my life! (*Applause.*)

PAULINE. Now, don't forget tomorrow afternoon is the fifth lesson in the Hustle series. There is still time to sign up. And now, boys and girls, let's dance good night. (*Music starts.*)

EMILY. (*At mic.*) If anyone finds an earring on the floor, it's mine.

(*As* NATHAN *and* MARLENE *sing "GOOD NIGHT"—the Stardust* REGULARS *dance the last dance.*)

GOOD NIGHT

NATHAN and MARLENE.
THE NIGHT IS ALMOST OVER
WE'VE NO MORE SONGS TO SPEND.
THERE'S ONLY TIME FOR ONE MORE DANCE.
ALL GOOD THINGS MUST END.
WE CAN'T HOLD BACK TOMORROW
NO MATTER HOW WE TRY.

BUT IT HELPS IF WE REMEMBER

GOOD NIGHT IS NOT GOODBYE.

OUTSIDE BEA'S HOUSE

BEA. (*Amused.*) Did he really say, "joined at the hip"? I was so close to the band, I couldn't hear.

AL. (*Chuckling.*) Well, you know, he's got to say something. (*They stop at the door.*)

BEA. (*Offering her hand.*) Al, I had a wonderful time.

AL. The best, so far.

BEA. Well . . . good night. And thank you.

AL. (*Releasing her hand reluctantly.*) Good night. (*A pause, then:*)

BEA. Would you like a cup of coffee?

AL. (*Grins.*) For a month now.

BEA. Please come in. (*They enter.*)

BEA'S LIVING ROOM

BEA. Well . . . this is it.

AL. It's nice.

BEA. Thank you.

AL. It's big.

BEA. Yes.

AL. Lovely.

BEA. Thank you. A lot of memories here.

AL. Bea?

BEA. Yes.

AL. Your Tango tonight, it was first class.

BEA. Shirley Selwyn's was better.

AL. I don't know about that. All I know is that you're the best partner I ever had . . . It's a great place, isn't it?

BEA. The Ballroom?

AL. Yeah.

BEA. I love it.

AL. Where else can I go for three dollars and be tall and handsome?

BEA. Well, ah, I'll just go and put on the coffee. (*She leaves for the kitchen.* AL *looks around the room.*)

AL. Bea? Oh, Bea?

BEA. Yes?

AL. Who made this thing.

BEA. Which?

AL. The blanket!

BEA. (*Entering.*) Oh, that's an afghan! I made that.

AL. It's beautiful.

BEA. It's easy. I used to do alot of crocheting before I went into business.

AL. I wish I had some talents.

BEA. Oh, you're a wonderful dancer. No, that's a talent.

AL. Did you ever go to college, Bea?

BEA. Me? No.

AL. Me neither. I went to the Army instead.

BEA. You were in the Army?

AL. Sure. World War II. You're lookin' at a war hero.

BEA. I bet you looked wonderful in your uniform.

AL. Well . . . so and so, you know. I got some pictures I'll bring them some time, and you'll judge for yourself.

BEA. Good! You look comfortable.

AL. I am. Very.

BEA. You know, Maury would have liked you, Al.

AL. You think so.

BEA. I know so. You're a good man, Al.

AL. I'm a different person since I met you, Bea. It's like how I feel now when I wake up in the morning. I'm so, well, I don't know if I can find the right words . . .

BEA. Well, it's just as well. You're embarrassing me.

AL. I'm sorry, I . . .

BEA. I'll just go see about the coffee. (*She goes back to the kitchen. AL watches her out.*)

AL. "My glass shall not persuade me I am old,
So long as youth and thou are of one date."

BEA. (*Calls.*) What?

AL. It's a sonnet by Shakespeare. Here's another one:
"Shall I compare thee to a summer's day?
Thou art more lovely and more temperate . . ."

BEA. (*Entering with coffee.*) My goodness, you certainly know your Shakespeare. How do you take your coffee?

AL. Black. The only way for a true coffee lover.

BEA. (*Serving.*) Or if you're on a diet, like me.

AL. You? What are you on a diet for?

BEA. Oh, boy, that's a good one!

AL. Oh, come on, Bea. You got a great shape.

BEA. Yeah, if you like pears.

AL. No, really . . . Bea . . . (AL *touches her shoulder.*)

BEA. Al, drink your coffee and go home. We both have to get up early in the morning.

AL. You look so lovely. (*He touches her hair. It leads to a kiss. When it lingers too long, BEA breaks away.*)

BEA. You better go, Al.

AL. I didn't mean to offend you, Bea.

BEA. (*Rising from couch.*) Offend me? I'm flattered. Really. It's just I'm not ready for this. (*She crosses toward the door.*)

AL. Can I kiss you good night?

BEA. You just did.

AL. Once more . . . please?

BEA. Well, if you want to . . . kiss me.

AL. (*After he kisses her.*) I love the way you look.

BEA. (*Extending her hand.*) Goodnight, Al.

AL. (*Starts to leave, turns.*) Good night. I had a wonderful time.

BEA. (*Shaking his hand.*) Oh, me, too.

AL. Good night.

BEA. Good night. (AL *is gone.*)

JUNK STORE

HELEN *is at the counter on the phone.* ELEANOR *is browsing.*

HELEN. Jack, believe me, there's nothing to worry about. Everybody gets palpitations. My heart stops a hundred times a day. (*She sees* ELEANOR *inspecting a small china figure.*) Hold on, Jack. (*To* ELEANOR.) Yes, can I help you?

ELEANOR. I was wondering . . . Is this genuine?

HELEN. Genuine what?

ELEANOR. I mean is it only what it is, or is it a copy of something else?

HELEN. It's only what it is.

ELEANOR. I thought that's what it was. (*Putting figure down.*) Thank you.

(HELEN *smiles politely.* ELEANOR *resumes browsing.*)

HELEN. (*Into phone.*) Listen, Jack, I've got people here. A mob. Stop worrying, will you? You're making yourself sick over your health. I'll see you home. (*She hangs up.*)

ELEANOR. Are the piano rolls in? I don't see them anywhere.

HELEN. What piano rolls?

ELEANOR. Bea told me she bought a collection at auction. She said they'd be in this week.

HELEN. Well, she didn't tell me about them, but then there's a lot she doesn't tell me these days.

(KATHY, *an attractive young woman, enters from the back wearing a stylish dress.*)

KATHY. (*To* ELEANOR.) Mother, what do you think? Don't you love it? (KATHY *observes herself in the mirror as* BEA *enters from the back.*)

BEA. I thought it might need shortening, Eleanor, but I think it's just fine.

ELEANOR. Turn around, Kathy, let me see.

BEA. You know I wore that dress when I was dating my husband. It was considered a Joan Crawford style then. My husband said it looked better on me than on Joan Crawford.

KATHY. Do you think it's me?

BEA. I think it looks better on you than on me or Joan.

ELEANOR. Kathy? (KATHY *nods enthusiastically*.) How much is it?

BEA. Well, it's marked thirty dollars. (*Seeing* ELEANOR'S *slight frown*.) Is that too much?

ELEANOR. For the dress, no; just for me it is, a little.

BEA. What would you like it to be?

HELEN. It's a real steal at thirty dollars.

BEA. How much can you afford?

ELEANOR. (*Hesitantly*.) Twenty dollars?

BEA. Sold.

ELEANOR. Really?

BEA. It's yours.

KATHY. (*Hugging* ELEANOR.) Oh, mom, thank you!

HELEN. (*To* BEA *at counter*.) Twenty dollars for a Joan Crawford original?

BEA. Helen, it's not an original.

HELEN. Neither is going out of business.

BEA. (*Crossing to* ELEANOR.) Eleanor, I'm going to leave you with Helen. I've got an appointment.

ELEANOR. (*Kissing* BEA'S *cheek*.) Thanks a million, sweetheart. I'll see you tonight.

(*As* BEA *rushes past her for the bag,* HELEN *speaks*.)

HELEN. What appointment . . . BEA! (BEA *doesn't answer. Exits.* HELEN *looks over at* KATHY, *looking at her new dress in the mirror*.) If you want it wrapped you'll have to take it off.

KATHY. Mom, I think I'll wear it home.

ELEANOR. Whatever you like. (*Opening her bag, to* HELEN.) Twenty dollars, right?

HELEN. That's what your friend said. (*Taking the money*.) Thank you.

KATHY. Thank *you*.

ELEANOR. Have a nice day.

HELEN. Not a chance.

(ELEANOR *and* KATHY *exit, as* DIANE *enters*.)

DIANE. Hello, Aunt Helen.

HELEN. Diane! You're just in time! She's on her way out.

DIANE. Out where?

HELEN. Do I know? Everytime I see her she's not there.

(BEA *re-enters with her coat.*)

BEA. Diane!

DIANE. Are you going someplace?

BEA. Oh, I wish I'd known you were coming. I've got an appointment and I can't be late.

DIANE. Mother, do you know what day this is?

BEA. It's Friday. (*Beat.*) Isn't it?

DIANE. Friday, the what?

BEA. Friday, the I-don't-know . . . what is it?

DIANE. It's the 18th, Mother. Friday, the 18th.

BEA. Did I forget to do something? Is it somebody's birthday?

DIANE. Tonight's the big dinner. Louis' firm. You promised to sit with the girls.

BEA. My God, this must be the 18th!

DIANE. You and I are going to have lunch today, remember? Then I'm going to drive you out to the Island.

BEA. Honey, I can't. I know I said I would, but I can't.

DIANE. What do you mean?

BEA. Helen, what about you? Can you do it? You don't care where you watch Jack sleep, do you?

HELEN. I can't. Not tonight. Jack's gotta take an upper G.I. in the morning.

DIANE. (*Annoyed.*) Mother, I don't understand. This was all arranged.

BEA. What about Becky next door? You can always get her and she's wonderful with the girls.

DIANE. That's not the idea.

BEA. And I'll pay for it.

DIANE. Moth-er.

BEA. Isn't that fair?

DIANE. I just don't know how you could forget.

BEA. Honey. I guess I've just got a lot of other things on my mind.

DIANE. I guess so. Do you know we haven't seen you in over a month?

HELEN. You wanna see your mother these days, you gotta buy a dance ticket.

DIANE. I'm sorry, Aunt Helen, I think maybe this should be private.

BEA. Uh . . . take a break, Helen. Go in the back, have a cup of coffee.

HELEN. Go in the back? What am I—the "help"? (*She goes in the back.*)

DIANE. The girls miss you, Mama.

BEA. I know. I miss them, too. But I speak to them on the phone.

DIANE. The phone is not their grandma.

BEA. Alright. Friday, I'll close the store and I'll meet Louis in the city and I'll come out for the weekend, alright?

DIANE. That's next weekend?

BEA. Yes.

DIANE. But you're really going to mess me up tonight.

BEA. And I've offered to make it right.

DIANE. But not by coming with me.

BEA. Diane, I can't. Not tonight.

DIANE. You still haven't told me why.

BEA. I've got a date.

DIANE. A date?

BEA. Yes.

DIANE. Another one?

BEA. How many am I allowed?

DIANE. And you can't break . . . your date?

BEA. Diane, I don't want to. Not this one or any other. (*Going to her.*) Sweetheart, something wonderful is happening to me. Now, please. Don't hold it against me! (BEA *leaves.*)

BALLROOM

COUPLES *are dancing the Rhumba.* AL *sits alone.*

I'VE BEEN WAITING ALL MY LIFE

NATHAN.
I'VE BEEN WAITING ALL MY LIFE
AND LOOKING FOR THE SMILE
THAT SAYS THE RAIN IS OVER.

I'VE BEEN LISTENING ALL MY LIFE
TO HEAR IN ONE "HELLO"
THE QUIET VOICE OF LOVE.

I'VE BEEN WAITING ALL MY LIFE FOR YOU;
LOOKING FOR THE DOOR THAT YOU'D COME
    THROUGH.

WANTING, WISHING ALL ALONG—
A SINGER WITH A SONG,
AND NO ONE TO SING IT TO!

ALL THE SONGS I'VE NEVER SUNG,
WITH WORDS I'VE NEVER USED,
YOU'RE HEARING WHEN I HOLD YOU.

AND NOW MY ARMS ARE OPEN WIDE,
THERE'S SO MUCH LOVE INSIDE—
YOU'LL NEVER WANT FOR MORE!

THE WAITING SEEMS SO LONG AGO.
YOU'RE HERE, MY LOVE AND OH,
WERE YOU WORTH WAITING FOR!

(EMILY *and* MARIO *dance by.*)

MARIO. Hey, Al, how's it going? Cume sta?
AL. Mezza, mezz.
EMILY. Hi, Al.

(ANGIE *and* LIGHTFEET *dance by.*)

AL. Hi, Emily. You're lookin' good.
EMILY. Oh, thank you.
AL. Angie, is Bea alright? She should be here by now.
ANGIE. (*A secret up her sleeve.*) Oh, I wouldn't worry about it if I were you.
AL. Well, when I talked to her before, she didn't say anything about being late.
ANGIE. Junk store ladies can be *very* mysterious.

(AL *sits on banquette again.* BILL *steps to* LIGHTFEET *and* ANGIE.)

BILL. Lightfeet, you gotta phone call.
LIGHTFEET. Now?
BILL. Some guy wants to talk to you.
LIGHTFEET. Take his number, okay?
BILL. SHE says it's very important.
LIGHTFEET. I'm sorry, babe. Gimme a minute.
ANGIE. Have I got a choice? (LIGHTFEET *goes Off.* ANGIE

crosses to AL. *They are the only two not dancing. To* AL.) It's murder being so popular, huh?

AL. (*Smiles.*) Yeah.

ANGIE. Okay, kid. On your feet. (*Holds her arms out for dancing.*) Take me to the Moon. (AL *joins her and they dance. After a bit,* AL *speaks.*)

AL. You know, Angie, this is the first time you and I ever danced together?

ANGIE. (*Distracted.*) Yeah, that's right. Look, I know your mind's on Bea, but try to pretend you're not holding a bag of groceries.

AL. (*Smiling.*) I'm sorry. (*He loosens up and holds her closer as they continue to dance.*)

ANGIE. Ridiculous, ain't it? A woman my age, and I still need a babysitter.

AL. Angie, is anything gonna happen with you and Lightfeet?

ANGIE. I don't think so. Some men are born married y'know?

AL. Yeah.

ANGIE. . . . Heaven help the outside lady.

(LIGHTFEET *returns, taps* AL's *shoulder.*)

LIGHTFEET. Thanks, Al. (AL *releases* ANGIE.)

AL. Oh. Okay.

ANGIE. Don't worry. She'll be here.

AL. I'm sure. Thank you.

(LIGHTFEET *and* ANGIE *resume dancing.*)

ANGIE. Everything alright?

LIGHTFEET. She told me to drop dead.

ANGIE. Finish the dance first.

NATHAN.

AND NOW MY ARMS ARE OPEN WIDE,
THERE'S SO MUCH LOVE INSIDE—
YOU'LL NEVER WANT FOR MORE!
THE WAITING SEEMS SO LONG AGO
YOU'RE HERE MY LOVE AND OH,
WERE YOU WORTH WAITING FOR.

BILL. (*At the entrance.*) Hey, gang! Believe it or not, here comes Bea . . .

(*The transformed* BEA *enters.*)

AL. Bea!
BEA. I'm sorry I'm late.
AL. What did you do?
ANGIE. Bea!
LIGHTFEET. Bea?
BEA. (*Worried.*) Is it alright?

(*As the* NEXT GROUP OF PEOPLE *pay compliments to* BEA, *her main concern is for* AL'S *reaction to her new look.*)

PETEY. Your hair!
MARTHA. And that dress!
BEA. Margaret helped me pick it out. Do you like it?
MARTHA. Oh, I really do?
ANGIE. You look gorgeous!
LIGHTFEET. You are a real knockout!
ANGIE. Oh, Beverly did good, Bea!
BEA. Yeah? Not too much?
AL. Dance, beautiful?
BEA. Honest, Al?
SHIRLEY. Oh, my God, Bea! Is that really you?
BEA. I'm not sure.
PAUL. Pret-ty la-dy!
BEA. Thank you.
HARRY. Bea Asher, you look enchanting!
BEA. Oh, Noodle!
ELEANOR. Love your hair, Bea.
NOODLE. Thank you.
SCOOTER. Cutting in, Al! (*He dances* BEA *away.*) Bea! You look incredible.
BEA. Now tell me. What happened?
SCOOTER. It went through!
BEA. Oh, Scooter, congratulations! That's wonderful!
SCOOTER. *You're* wonderful, Bea! (*He kisses her. She returns to* AL.)
RUSS. (*Dancing past with* CHRISTINA.) All-*right*!
BEA. Where were we?
AL. What was that all about with Scooter?
BEA. Nothing.
AL. What did he want?

BEA. He just wanted to thank me for something.

AL. Thank you for what? And did he have to thank you so close?

BEA. Al, I co-signed a loan so he could go back into business.

AL. You're beautiful! Inside and out you're beautiful!

BILL. (*Walking past.*) Bea, fantastic! Fantastic!

BEA. Thank you, Bill.

MARGARET. Bea, perfect!

(BEA *and* AL *laugh, as* MARGARET *glides off.*)

AL. Bea!

BEA. Al!

BEA. (*To* AL.) You don't think I look foolish?

AL. You look like a movie star!

BEA. A movie star! (*Laughs.*) Which one?

AL. All of them! (*They both laugh and embrace, begin to dance and sing.*)

I LOVE TO DANCE

AL.
I LOVE TO DANCE EV'RY SINGLE DANCE
WHEN I'M HOLDING YOU IN MY ARMS.
NO NEED TO SPEAK—
JUST CHEEK TO CHEEK—
TWO PEOPLE LIGHT AS A FEATHER,
WE'RE EVEN BREATHING TOGETHER.
AND AS WE TRAVEL ACROSS THE FLOOR,
SEEMS IT'S MORE LIKE FLOATING ON AIR.
COME AND DANCE WITH ME,
YOU AND I CAN BE GINGER RODGERS AND FRED
    ASTAIRE!
TELL THE BAND TO BLOW EV'RY TUNE THEY KNOW
AND THROW IN A TANGO OR TWO.
HOW I LOVE TO DANCE, EV'RY SINGLE DANCE
WHEN THE GIRL IN MY ARMS IS YOU!
BEA.
I LOVE TO DANCE EV'RY SINGLE DANCE
WHEN YOU'RE HOLDING ME IN YOUR ARMS.
EV'RY GIRL NEEDS
SOMEONE WHO LEADS—

NO HARM FORGETTIN' THE SWEET TALK—
WHEN WE ARE LETTIN' OUR FEET TALK.
WHENEVER I HEAR THE MUSIC START
BABY, YOU'RE THE PARTNER I CHOOSE—
YOU WERE BORN TO BE
CHEEK TO CHEEK WITH ME—
ARTHUR MURRAY CAN'T SHINE YOUR SHOES!
'ROUND AND 'ROUND WE GO—IS THERE GROUND
   BELOW?
THIS FEELING'S TOO GOOD TO BE TRUE!
HOW I LOVE TO DANCE EV'RY SINGLE DANCE
WHEN THE MAN IN MY ARMS IS YOU!

LIMBO

*They continue to dance and they kiss, long and passionately.
   The kiss ends.*

AL. If thou could but know how much I feel for thee . . .
BEA. William Shakespeare.
AL. No, Al Rossi. I just made it up.
BEA. Honest to God.
AL. Honest to God.
BEA. I'm so impressed! (*They kiss again. She takes his hand
and leads him away.*)
AL. (*Stops, turns. He is crying.*) Bea . . . I'm married. (*A long
pause.*)
BEA. (*Almost to herself.*) I knew.
AL. (*Frowning.*) I never said a word.
BEA. That's what told me.
AL. I was afraid if I did I'd lose you. (*Pause.*) She and I—
BEA. (*She silences him with a gesture.*) I don't want to know
anything about it . . . ever. (*She takes AL's hand.*)

BEA'S LIVING ROOM

*AL is alone, studying a Scrabble board with great concentration.
   He takes six tiles from his rack and places them on the board.*

AL. A.B.L.E. (*Calls.*) O.K., Bea. Come on! It's your turn.
(*He takes five new letters and places them on his rack.*)
BEA. (*Calls.*) I'm just getting you some dessert.

AL. I don't really need it.

BEA. (*Entering with a powdered coffee ring.*) No, you'll love it.

AL. I just made 42 points.

BEA. 42?? (*Looking at the board.*) Al . . . Al. What is that?

AL. "Gullable."

BEA. "Gullable" isn't spelled with an "A" it's spelled with an "I."

AL. Either spelling is acceptable.

BEA. Who says?

AL. It's your turn. (BEA *goes to the bookcase, takes a dictionary, returns to the couch, sits, opens it, finds the word, reads, loses the battle, closes the dictionary, and returns it to the shelf.* AL, *all the while, hums smugly.*) Come on, it's your turn.

BEA. It's not fair. It looks so wrong.

AL. Oh, come on, Bea. The board is wide open.

BEA. It doesn't matter. I've got lousy letters.

AL. Look, you've got a triple word score here, and a double here . . .

BEA. It doesn't matter. I'm telling you, I've got lousy letters—

AL. Like what?

BEA. Oh, no. You're not going to trick me into telling you what I've got.

AL. Maybe I can help you.

BEA. I don't need any help.

AL. Well, you are pretty slow.

BEA. Yes. I'm slow. You know why?

AL. Why?

BEA. Because you put pressure on me, you make me nervous, and then I can't concentrate.

AL. I put pressure on you?

BEA. Yes, you do. See, you're doing it right now. Now watch this.

AL. Go ahead.

BEA. (*Fiercely, she takes one letter after another and lays them on the board.*) R-A-T-S! Rats! There! . . . How much do I get?

AL. Rats! That's it!?

BEA. Yeah.

AL. It's only four points.

BEA. Don't I get a double word score?

AL. Bea, you need at least a five-letter word.

BEA. Oh.

AL. See, now, if you had a "t."

BEA. I don't have a "t."

AL. Well, if you had an "e"?

BEA. Al, I don't have an "E." I don't need any help!

AL. Okay, then I go.

BEA. Right. Go.

AL. Okay. I'm using these four letters here, and I'm adding five of my own. You watching?

BEA. I'm watching.

AL. A-D-O-R-A-B-I-L-E.

BEA. Adora BILE! What's that!

AL. That's thirty-seven points.

BEA. Is that a real word?

AL. Absolutely.

BEA. What does it mean?

AL. Adorable.

BEA. Al, "adorable" doesn't have an "I."

AL. In Italian it does.

BEA. Only English in this game, Mister.

AL. (*Romantically.*) Adorabile, adorabile, adorabile!

BEA. Oh . . . Okay . . . just this once. But from now on English only.

AL. It's your turn.

BEA. I've got to pick new tiles.

AL. (*Rising.*) Please, be my guest.

BEA. Where are you goin'?

AL. I'm going to get a piece of cake.

BEA. (*Frowning as she picks new tiles.*) This is hopeless.

AL. (*Sampling the cake.*) This is delicious. Delicious. Did you bake it.

BEA. Bake! Who has time to bake?

AL. (*Looking over her shoulder.*) Oh, Bea. Watch. Oh, Bea, watch. This is fantastic.

BEA. No, Al . . . I don't want . . . No, Al!

AL. (*Leans over, takes her tiles one-by-one, all seven of them, and lays them on the board.*) F-O-X-T-R-O-T-S. Foxtrots. That's fifty points for using all your letters, plus the triple word score, and double letter score for using your "F."

BEA. (*Totaling her score on the score sheet.*) Okay, I win. I don't wanna play anymore.

AL. What happened. I was winning.

BEA. I'm too good for you. (*They laugh and embrace.*)

AL. Oh, Bea, Bea. I love you so much. (*He pulls her to him, hugs her.*)

BEA. I love you, too. (*A new thought.*) Al. Is that short for Albert or Alfred? Y'know, I've never asked.

AL. Alfred. Well, really Alfredo. In case I haven't mentioned it, my mother and father were Italian.

BEA. I wish I'd known them.

AL. They were beautiful people. My father used to drive a truck. To my mother he was a king. You know something? (*Touching her cheek.*) For the first time in my life, I think I know how they felt about each other.

BEA. That's a lovely compliment.

AL. Well, we'd have to go a long way to beat them. They were married fifty-two years. (*It's a bad word to have used.*) I'm sorry, Bea.

BEA. (*She turns on the radio.*) Hey, how do you say "dance" in Italian?

AL. *Ballare.*

BEA. Okay, *Adorabile,* come on and *ballare* with me!

AL. The Hustle?

BEA. Yes. We spent all that money on lessons, we shouldn't let it go to waste.

AL. Why not. Okay. Left foot first?

BEA. Right.

AL. Right?

BEA. My right, your left. Let's start with the Basic: step, step, point . . . step, step, point . . . 1, 2, 3, 1, 2, 3, 1, 2, 3—

AL. Macho!

(*They dance,* AL *in his stockinged feet, jacket off, his shirt open at the neck;* BEA *in a hostess gown.* HELEN *enters and stops short, stunned to see the redhead in a strange man's arms in this romantic setting. It is a moment before* BEA *notices her.*)

BEA. Oh! My God, Helen! You scared me to death!

HELEN. I rang, I knocked, but the music was so loud, so I used my key.

BEA. This is my sister-in-law, Helen. Helen, this is Al Rossi.

AL. (*Extending his hand.*) How do you do? Pleased to meet you.

(HELEN *shakes his hand.* BEA *turns off the radio, puts up the light.*)

HELEN. Yes, thank you. Jack and I went to the Pink Pagoda. We thought you'd like some duck.

BEA. No, thank you, we've— (*Self-conscious about the noun.*)—had dinner already.

HELEN. Oh. What did you fix?

BEA. I—ah—

AL. She made the veal, I made the pasta. I do a fantastic rigatoni.

HELEN. I bet you do.

AL. I'm glad I've had the opportunity to meet you, Helen. Bea has spoken a lot about you.

BEA. Yes.

HELEN. Yes?

BEA. Yes.

AL. She tells me what a big help you are to her in the store.

HELEN. Thank you.

BEA. Helen, if you're going to stay, take off your coat.

HELEN. Jack wants to say hello, when he finds a place to park.

(*Silence,* AL *goes to chair and picks up his jacket.*)

BEA. Oh, are you leaving?

AL. Yeh, I'd better. It's getting late, and we all have to be at work in the morning. (*Puts on his jacket.*) See you at the Ballroom?

BEA. Yes.

AL. Good night. (*He goes to kiss her, stops himself, extends his hand.*)

BEA. (*Takes it.*) Good night, Al.

AL. (*To* HELEN.) Good night, Helen.

HELEN. Good night. (AL *exits.*)

BEA. Helen, Helen, why didn't you call first?

HELEN. I'm shocked at you, Bea! What is going on here? What have you done to yourself?

BEA. What do you mean, what have I done to myself?

HELEN. Your hair! Your new dresses! You can see everything you've got in them. Bea, for heaven sakes, you're a grandmother!

BEA. Helen, I like the way I look!

HELEN. Do you know that the whole neighborhood is talking?! Men coming into your house, leaving at all hours?

BEA. Only one man, Helen.

HELEN. Is this a serious relationship, Bea?

BEA. Well, of course it's serious. I wouldn't know how to have any other kind of a relationship.

HELEN. Are you going to marry him?

BEA. No.

HELEN. No? In other words, you are having an affair?

BEA. Go home, Helen.

HELEN. It's disgraceful! It's an insult to the memory of my brother—

BEA. (*Cuts in firmly.*) Helen, I want you to go home.

HELEN. I just don't understand, Bea.

(JACK *enters.*)

JACK. I finally found a place.

HELEN. Jack . . .

JACK. (*Sighs.*) Don't tell me. We're leaving. (HELEN *leaves with* JACK.)

BALLROOM

NATHAN. Alright, Boys and Girls. Let's put all those Hustle lessons together!

MORE OF THE SAME

MARLENE.
I DON'T KNOW WHAT FOREVER IS—
AND I JUST KNOW TOMORROW BY NAME.
BUT NOW IS HERE AND WONDERFUL
AND I ONLY WANT MORE OF THE SAME.
NATHAN and MARLENE.
I ONLY WANT MORE OF THE MOMENTS
WHEN WE'RE ALONE IN THE WORLD LIKE THIS—
NOT LOOKING BACK AT YESTERDAY
OR BEYOND THE VERY NEXT KISS.
NATHAN.
I WANT NOTHING MORE THAN TO LOOK AT YOU
AND TO FIND YOU LOOKING AT ME.
NOW THAT I'VE SEEN THE LOVE IN YOUR EYES.
NATHAN and MARLENE.
WHAT ELSE IS THERE TO SEE?

WHAT ELSE DO I NEED BUT ONE DAY AT A TIME?
ONE DREAM AT A TIME TO COME TRUE?
WHAT ELSE DO I DO?
NOTHING MORE—
THAN MORE OF THE SAME WITH YOU.
    MARLENE.
MORE, MORE, GIMME MORE,
MORE, GIMME MORE OF THE SAME.
    NATHAN and MARLENE.
MORE, MORE, GIMME MORE,
MORE, GIMME MORE OF THE SAME.

MORE, MORE, GIMME MORE
MORE, GIMME MORE OF THE SAME—
GIMME, GIMME, GIMME.

MORE, MORE, MORE, MORE, MORE,
GIMME ALL YOU GOT!

(*Dance break.*)

    MARLENE.
I WANT IT—
I NEED IT—
YOU GOT IT—
GIVE IT TO ME BABY!
    NATHAN.
MORE . . .
    MARLENE.
I WANT IT!
    NATHAN.
MORE . . .
    MARLENE.
I NEED IT!
    NATHAN.
MORE . . .
    MARLENE.
YOU GOT IT!
    NATHAN and MARLENE.
GOTTA HAVE IT BABY!

MORE—MORE—MORE—MORE—MORE—MORE

WHAT ELSE DO I NEED BUT ONE DAY AT A TIME?
ONE DREAM AT A TIME TO COME TRUE?
WHY SHOULD I SETTLE FOR ANYTHING LESS,
THAN

MORE OF THE SAME
MORE OF THE SAME
MORE OF THE SAME
MORE—OF THE SAME!

MORE OF THE SAME
MORE OF THE SAME
MORE OF THE SAME
MORE—OF THE SAME!

MORE OF THE SAME
MORE OF THE SAME
MORE OF THE SAME
MORE—OF THE SAME!

MORE OF THE SAME
MORE OF THE SAME
MORE OF THE SAME

—WITH YOU . . . !

(BEA *crosses the dance floor.* COUPLES *are congratulating each other. A fanfare announces* QUEEN PAULINE, *who goes to the center of the dance floor.*)

PAULINE. Okay, everybody. I've saved the best till last. Next Saturday night we will be crowning our new Queen of the Stardust Ballroom. (*Applause. Comments.*) And, here to make the first of our nominating speeches is one of our oldest regulars. Miss Emily Vogel!
EMILY. Thank you. Where does she get that "oldest" stuff? (*Laughter. Reading.*) The woman that I wish to place in— (*Struggling.*)—that I—Oh, the hell with it! I'll try it from memory. (*Without notes.*) This lady came to the Ballroom as my guest seven years ago. She's never missed a night of dancing—except for the month in 1972, when she had her nose job. Ha, ha . . . only kidding, Marie. Oh, Jeez! I gave it away!

Anyhow, she helped with the Raffle Sale and she did a terrific job
with the Halloween decorations, so I hereby place in nomination a
very fine person, and a very good friend—Marie Kalowicz!

(*A scream from* MARIE. *Cheers, applause, music.* FRIENDS *congratulate* MARIE.)

PAULINE. Good luck next Saturday night, Marie.
MARIE. Thank you.
PAULINE. Our second nominating speech is by a former queen
herself. The ever-lovely Eleanor Martin.

(*Applause. Wold whistles.*)

ELEANOR. Thank you all. A woman of character. A woman of
taste. A sensitive woman. A generous woman. A woman who's
had her share of pain but a woman who knows how to derive
pleasure. A woman of energy. A woman of spirit. A *woman* for
all seasons. Our second nominee—Miss Shirley Selwin.

(*Applause. Cheers. Music.* SHIRLEY *hyperventilates.*)

LIGHTFEET. (*Crossing to* BEA.) I called Al's house, Bea.
BEA. (*Grateful, anxious.*) Yes?
LIGHTFEET. No answer. No one's at home.
BEA. Oh. (BEA, *dejected, goes to the banquette*)
PAULINE. Good luck, Shirley.
SHIRLEY. Thank you, Pauline.
PAULINE. Our final nominating speech is by the Lindy Champion of the Ballroom and she's just about as nice a gal as they
come. Miss Angie O'Hara!

(*Applause.* ANGIE *struts Center.*)

ANGIE. Okay, you guys! I been waitin' five years for someone
to nominate *me*. I'm beginnin' to get an inferiority complex.
LIGHTFEET. Wait'll next year, Angie!
ANGIE. *This* year was next year, Sweetheart. (*Laughter.*) Kidding aside, what can I tell ya' about this person that tells you
everything I feel about her in my heart. A year ago when she first
came here with me, there was enough sadness about her to fill
the room. I'd kept pestering her about the Stardust—in my own

sweet way—and finally she took a chance. She found the courage to stop livin' in the past and to take a try at a future. We've all watched this lady blossom. She's showed us what we're all capable of. This lady runs a very successful business she built all by herself. This lady has a son, who is a professor of English in California! This lady, whose name I now place in nomination, is my friend and yours—Bea Asher!

(*Applause. Cheers, music.*)

PAULINE. Congratulations and good luck next Saturday night, Bea. (ANGIE *hugs* BEA *who, deeply emotional, hugs her* FRIEND.) And now, it's time for the Dance of the Nominees! Get your partners, girls!

BEA. My partner's not here.

LIGHTFEET. (*Calls.*) Hey, Harry! (HARRY *comes over.*) One of the nominees here needs a partner. (*He indicates* BEA.)

BEA. I'm right back where I started.

HARRY. It's my good fortune.

(*They dance among the* OTHERS. PEOPLE *begin leaving the Ballroom. The Stardust sign lowers and* COUPLES *begin to exit the Ballroom. Among those we see are* MARTHA *and* PETEY *with* FAY *and* SCOOTER.)

MARTHA. Good night, you two.

FAY and SCOOTER. Good night, Martha. So long.

PETEY. (*Overlapping.*) Take care.

MARTHA. (*Kissing* FAY'S *cheek.*) See you tomorrow?

FAY. I'm sitting for my daughter. She's workin' on getting married again.

MARTHA. You're a doll.

PETEY. Seeya.

(MARTHA *and* PETEY *go off in one direction.* FAY *and* SCOOTER *start off in the other.*)

SCOOTER. Hey, wait. I'll walk you to the bus.

FAY. You're all heart. (*They go off, as* BEA, ANGIE *and* LIGHTFEET *exit Ballroom.*)

LIGHTFEET. You girls wait here. I'll get the car. (*He leaves.*

BEA's *mind is on the absent* AL *and* ANGIE *does her best to distract her.*)

ANGIE. Did the Noodle tell you about the matches?

BEA. No, I don't think so.

ANGIE. He's gonna have 'em printed up where he works, on the cover it'll say "Bea For Queen."

BEA. (*Smiles.*) He's not.

ANGIE. Oh, yeah, he said. I told ya to stick with me. (*With hand gesture.*) Already I've got your name up in matches.

(EMILY *and* MARIO *exit Ballroom.*)

MARIO. Good night, ladies.

EMILY. Good night.

ANGIE. So long, guys.

BEA. Good night.

(*As* BEA *and* ANGIE *say their goodbyes,* AL *enters. As* EMILY *and* MARIO *pass him:*)

MARIO. Ciao, Al.

AL. Ciao, Mario . . . Emily. (EMILY *and* MARIO *exit.* AL *crosses to* BEA *and* ANGIE.) I'm glad I caught you. Hi, Angie.

ANGIE. Hi.

AL. I'm sorry, Bea.

ANGIE. *Queen* Bea to you, pal.

AL. What?

ANGIE. I nominated her tonight.

AL. (*Pleased.*) No kiddin'!

ANGIE. It's between her and Marie and Shirley.

AL. (*Taking* BEA's *hand.*) My money's on Bea.

ANGIE. Oh, yeah. Marie's nice, but she's kinda blah and Shirley's startin' to sound like the goddam air conditioner. How do you wanna work goin' home, Bea? We can't all fit in Lightfeet's car.

AL. We'll be alright.

LIGHTFEET'S VOICE. (*Calls.*) Let's go, girls!

ANGIE. (*Calls.*) Okay! (*Going to* BEA.) You're a cinch, Bea. Queens don't get elected. They're born that way.

BEA. (*Touched.*) Angie. (BEA *hugs her.*)

ANGIE. Now, to join Mr. Right. Before he goes home to *Mrs.* Right. (*She exits. After a moment:*)

AL. (*Taking* BEA'S *hand.*) It was a family thing. I couldn't be in two places at one time.

BEA. It happens.

AL. I would have called if I could. (*Realizing.*) You're shaking. What's the matter?

BEA. I don't know how I held myself together tonight.

AL. I'd have done anything to spare you this upset.

BEA. Upset? (*Retrieving her hand.*) I didn't think you were just late. I was terrified you weren't coming at all.

AL. Would I do that to you? To us? Honey, I love you.

BEA. I felt so vulnerable. All the strength I thought I built up. Tonight was such a step backward for me.

AL. It won't happen again.

BEA. You know you can't promise that.

AL. No, not really.

BEA. I've been fooling myself, Al, saying that how it is doesn't matter. The truth is, I want you to be in only one place at a time. With me.

AL. I can't leave her. She's not the only one to blame for the way things are.

BEA. I know. But I need more. Maybe if I were younger. But I need to know that I can count on being with you. I can't crumble if you don't walk through a door. I won't go around being scared. It was almost easier being lonely. (*She starts to go.*)

AL. Bea.

BEA. I'll get home alright.

AL. Let me take you.

BEA. Let me go, Al.

AL. Bea . . .

BEA. Please. We've said it all. (*She leaves him.*)

BEA'S LIVING ROOM

Present are: HELEN, DIANE *and* DAVID. JACK, *in overcoat and hat, dozes in* MAURY'S *chair.*

HELEN. The point is, children, your mother is sleeping with a mailman! And she doesn't want to marry him.

DAVID. (*Touchily.*) Alright, Aunt Helen, we get the picture.

HELEN. As if it's not bad enough . . . he even *looks* like a mailman.

DAVID. What the hell does *that* mean?

HELEN. Wait, you'll see. They'll be here soon, the lovebirds.
DAVID. Aunt Helen, please!

(JACK *emits a short, loud snore.* HELEN *goes to him, shakes his shoulder.*)

HELEN. (*Annoyed.*) Jack, close your mouth when you sleep.

   (JACK *wakes with a start, not realizing where he is.*)

JACK. What? Huh? (*Yawning.*) What time is it?
DAVID. (*Checking his watch.*) Almost ten.
JACK. (*Puzzled.*) Ten?
HELEN. (*Checking her watch.*) Almost *one.*
DAVID. (*Realizing.*) Oh, I'm still on California time.
JACK. (*Relieved.*) Thank God! I thought it was tomorrow.
HELEN. One o'clock in the morning and our Cinderella's not home from the ball.
DIANE. (*Annoyed.*) Aunt Helen, when you talk like that it doesn't help anything at all.
HELEN. You think *I* like it?
BEA'S VOICE. Hello?
DIANE. (*Calls.*) Don' be scared, Ma. It's us.
BEA. (*Entering.*) What are you all—? (*Spotting him.*) David! David! (*Hugging him.*) What are you doing here? What's wrong? Is anybody sick? Where's Jennifer?
DIANE. Nobody's sick, Ma.
DAVID. Jennifer's in L.A.
BEA. Why didn't you tell me you were coming?
DAVID. I didn't know, Ma. It's kind of an emergency.
BEA. What? What's an emergency?
DAVID. I think it's you, Ma.
HELEN. Where's Senor Rossi? Aren't the kids going to meet him?
BEA. Oh, I see. I don't know where he is, Helen. (*To* HELEN.) You called David. What else did you tell him?
HELEN. The truth. Every single bit of it.
JACK. At a dollar a minute.
DAVID. Is it true, Ma? That you've suddenly got this whole new life at some ballroom? And that there's all this running around back here with a man?
BEA. "Running around?" Is that how she put it?

DIANE. Mama . . . are you going to marry him?

BEA. No, honey, I can't.

DAVID. Can we ask why?

BEA. . . . Because he's married already.

HELEN. What?

DIANE. Oh, God!

HELEN. Jack! Did you hear? He's a married man.

JACK. (*A sly grin at* BEA.) You son-of-a-gun.

HELEN. (*Glares at* JACK, *then.*) Bea, have you lost your mind?

DIANE. Is he going to get a divorce?

BEA. I don't discuss it with him; I'm not going to discuss it with you.

DIANE. You're just going to go on this way? You don't care?

BEA. Darling, how I go on is for *me* to decide.

HELEN. I thank God my brother's not alive now!

BEA. That's right, Helen. If Maury saw his widow behaving this way, it would probably kill him.

HELEN. Bea!

BEA. He is *not* alive! That's the whole point! And I am! And not just barely anymore, the way I was in the beginning. Did you all like it better when all I had were the four walls for company? Have you ever been in this house alone? Have you ever been *everywhere* alone? So I found a place to go. And another way to be. My God, I should think you'd be happy not to be burdened with me! I can tell you this: I don't want to be burdened by any of you anymore. I am nobody's emergency! In fact, some people think I'm pretty terrific! I don't want to come home to any more questions or opinions! I'm tired of these night raids! Helen— (*Puts out her hand.*) Turn in your key!!

HELEN. Come on, Diane. We promised to drive you home.

JACK. When did we promise to drive her home?

(HELEN'S *look silences him.*)

DIANE. Goodbye, David. Thanks for coming all this way. (*She and* DAVID *kiss.*)

JACK. (*Shaking hands.*) Goodbye, David. Get some sun.

DAVID. Goodbye, Uncle Jack.

HELEN. Goodbye, David. Make sure you sit in the back of the plane.

DIANE. Good night, Mama.

BEA. Good night, Diane.

DIANE. Mama . . . I hope he makes you very happy. (DIANE *exits.*)

BEA. (*Reflects on the thought; then, to* DAVID.) Well, David, how are you?

DAVID. Fine, Ma. Like your hair.

BEA. Thanks. How *is* Jennifer?

DAVID. Jennifer's pregnant, Ma. We're going to have a baby.

BEA. (*Thrilled.*) Oh, David! When? How long? (*They embrace.*)

DAVID. Middle of May, we think.

BEA. Oh, David, David.

DAVID. And we're gonna get married, Ma.

BEA. You didn't have to do that for me.

DAVID. You are something else, Ma. Let me go upstairs and shower, I'll tell you everything. Wait'll I tell you about California. You'll think I'm making it up. (BEA *laughs. Sincerely.*) And I want to hear all about you and him, Ma. You've got a good thing there, ugh?

BEA. Yes . . . I've got a very good thing . . . (*She sings.*)
I DON'T IRON HIS SHIRTS
I DON'T SEW ON HIS BUTTONS,
I DON'T KNOW ALL THE JOKES HE TELLS
OR THE SONGS HE HUMS.
THOUGH I MAY HOLD HIM
ALL THROUGH THE NIGHT,
HE MAY NOT BE HERE
WHEN THE MORNING COMES.

I DON'T PICK OUT HIS TIES
OR EXPECT HIS TOMORROWS,
BUT I FEEL WHEN HE'S IN MY ARMS
HE'S WHERE HE WANTS TO BE,
WE HAVE NO MEM'RIES
BITTERSWEET WITH TIME,
AND I DOUBT IF HE'LL SPEND
NEW YEARS EVE WITH ME.

I DON'T SHARE HIS NAME.
I DON'T WEAR HIS RING.
THERE'S NO PIECE OF PAPER
SAYING THAT HE'S MINE.
BUT HE SAYS HE LOVES ME

AND I BELIEVE IT'S TRUE
DOESN'T THAT MAKE SOMEONE
BELONG TO YOU?

SO I DON'T SHARE HIS NAME,
SO I DON'T WEAR HIS RING,
SO THERE'S NO PIECE OF PAPER
SAYING THAT HE'S MINE.
SO WE DON'T HAVE THE MEM'RIES
I HAVE ENOUGH MEM'RIES
I'VE WASHED ENOUGH MORNINGS,
I'VE DRIED ENOUGH EVENINGS,
I'VE HAD ENOUGH BIRTHDAYS,
TO KNOW WHAT I WANT.

LIFE IS ANYONE'S GUESS
IT'S A CONSTANT SURPRISE
THOUGH YOU DON'T PLAN TO FALL IN LOVE
WHEN YOU FALL YOU FALL.
I'D RATHER HAVE FIFTY PERCENT OF HIM,
OR ANY PERCENT OF HIM,
THAN ALL OF ANYBODY ELSE AT ALL!

BALLROOM

COUPLES *whirl on, in gowns and tuxedos. They spin and spin until the music stops.* BEA *and* AL *enter from different directions. Fanfare.*

NATHAN. Ladies and Gentlemen, it's the moment of the year. Please clear the dance floor. (COUPLES *clear.* MARLENE *holds crown on a pillow.*) I give you the reigning queen—Pauline Krim.

(*Music as* PAULINE *goes to the Bandstand. She no longer is wearing the crown.*)

PAULINE. Nathan, may I have the envelope, please? (NATHAN *hands it to her, she opens and reads it.*) Ladies and Gentlemen, the new Queen of the Stardust Ballroom is—Bea Asher.

(*Cheers and applause.* AL *escorts* BEA *toward* PAULINE. *He assists in the crowning.*)

BEA. This is such a great honor. I'm so happy. I'm *so happy*. How can I ever repay you? I wish I could say to everyone what someone said to me. "Come to the Ballroom," Angie used to say. "There's a terrific band and a real great crowd." "Come dancing," she said. And I said, "Dancing?" And she said, "Some people never go dancing."

I WISH YOU A WALTZ

BEA.
SOME PEOPLE NEVER GO DANCING
THEY DON'T HEAR THE MUSIC OF THE BAND.
SOME PEOPLE NEVER GO DANCING,
SO HOW CAN THEY UNDERSTAND?

TOO BAD YOU NEVER WENT DANCING
TOO BAD YOU NEVER HEARD THE BAND
I WISH YOU A WALTZ OR A CHA CHA CHA,
THEN MAYBE YOU'LL UNDERSTAND.

SOMEWHERE AN ORCHESTRA'S PLAYING—
MUSIC YOU'VE NEVER HEARD BEFORE.
SOMEWHERE THERE'S ALWAYS A WALTZ GOING ON,
WITH PLENTY OF ROOM ON THE FLOOR.

I WISH YOU A WALTZ
TO SEE HOW IT FEELS.
FOR ONCE IN YOUR LIFE
JUST KICK UP YOUR HEELS!
I WISH YOU A NIGHT
AND A MIRROR BALL . . .
I WISH YOU A WALTZ,
THAT'S ALL!

(AL *joins* BEA *and they begin to waltz.* ANGIE *and* LIGHTFEET *join them, followed by* OTHER COUPLES *until* EVERYONE *is* waltzing under the shining mirror ball. The lights fade as they dance on and on . . .)

THE END

COSTUME PLOT

ACT ONE, SCENE 1—Junkstore

DOROTHY LOUDON: Peach print duster over orchid print dress (for Ballroom I) beige suede low-heeled shoes, nude hose

SALLY-JANE HEIT: Gold & cream mini-check blouse (rigged for quick change) beige wrap skirt, brown loafers, nude hose, beige raincoat, brown purse

MARILYN COOPER: Brown/orange/yellow print skirt-top-vest, beige & black chanel pumps, brown purse

ROBERTA HAZE: Brown & cream checked skirt, Blue/green plaid shirt, Brown & green print headscarf, brown boots, brown purse

BARBARA ERWIN: Yellow/brown/cream plaid skirt, yellow sweater, Yellow print headscarf, taupe sling back pumps, nude hose, brown purse

PATRICIA DRYLIE: Green raincoat, green waitress uniform, pink hankie pinned to uniform, white apron, nude hose, white lace-up shoes

ACT ONE, SCENE 2—Ballroom entrance

DOROTHY LOUDON: Beige coat, Orchid print dress, (same hose and shoes as Junk 1) beige suede clutch purse, pearl necklace & earrings

MARY ANN NILES: Fur neckpiece over foxtrot dress

SVETLANA GRODY: Fur scarf over foxtrot dress

LIZ SHERIDEN: Green raincoat over foxtrot dress

ADRIANA KEATHLEY: Mauve knit shawl over foxtrot dress

MARILYN COOPER: Grey shawl over foxtrot dress

CAROL FLEMMING: Burgundy macrame shawl over foxtrot dress

MAVIS RAY: Fur stole over foxtrot dress

BARBARA ERWIN: Orchid feather boa over foxtrot dress

TERRY VIOLINO: Beige raincoat over foxtrot dress

DAVID EVANS: Beige raincoat over foxtrot suit

MICHAEL VITA: Grey plaid raincoat over foxtrot suit

JOHN MARTIN: Beige raincoat over foxtrot suit

JOE MILAN: Beige raincoat over foxtrot suit

PETER GLADKE: Taupe belted raincoat over foxtrot suit

GENE KELTON: Camel belted raincoat over foxtrot suit

ACT ONE, SCENE 3—Ballroom 1—"The Foxtrot"

DOROTHY LOUDON: Same dress as ACT ONE, SCENE 2 without coat and purse

VINCENT GARDENIA: Grey 2-pc. suit, blue & white striped shirt, blue & cream tie, black sox, black shoes

LYNN ROBERTS: Multi-color floor length sheath with multi-sparkles, black hose, silver sandals, earrings

BERNIE KNEE: Black tuxedo, White pleated shirt, black bow tie, black sox, black patent shoes

PATRICIA DRYLIE: Rust dress lined in green with purple flower, nude hose, rust shoes, rust earrings, green trunks, camel coat

HOWARD PARKER: Green sport coat with rust overplaid, reddish brown slacks, green plaid shirt, burgundy and beige striped tie, brown belt, beige & rust handkerchief, camel dotted sox, lt. brown shoes

BARBARA ERWIN: Greenish-grey and purple print chiffon dress, lined with purple, gold & rhinestone pin, gold earrings & bracelet, nude hose, brown shoes, boa

GENE KELTON: Green sport coat with rust & cream stripe, green & grey pants, pink shirt, burgundy & navy paisley tie, brown belt, burgundy hankie, black & white sox, brown shoes

LIZ SHERIDEN: Shades of green & burgundy print chiffon wrap dress lined with light green, nude hose, lt. beige laced shoes, jewelry

MICHAEL VITA: Brown & beige tweed suit with rust & blue overplaid, light orange striped shirt, brown with rust & cream tie, brown with rust hankie, brown & beige argyle sox, brown suede shoes, brown belt

JAYNE TURNER: Rose bat-wing sweater, lt. blue, cream, navy & reddish print skirt on net bodice, nude hose, lilac shoes, jewelry

DANNY CARROLL: Brown & rust textured suit, lt. orange shirt, beige & blue paisley tie, burgundy & grey hankie, burgundy & grey argyle sox, brown suede shoes, brown belt

JANET WHITE: Navy, camel & red print long torso dress, with dress clips, necklace, earrings, nude hose, nude shoes, tiara

ROBERTA HAZE: Lilac silk narrow pants, orchid knit halter top body suit, orchid and green print ruffled wrap skirt, nude hose, lavender suede shoes, jewels

VICTOR GRIFFIN: Dk & lt. brown tweed suit coat, brown & cream plaid pants, lavender shirt, brown/beige/cream tie, burgundy & cream hankie, brown belt, brown silky sox, reddish brown shoes

ADRIANA KEATHLEY: Rose, pale yellow & lilac print dress, with fuchsia camisole & ruffles, beige wide belt, nude hose, beige heels, jewels

MARY ANN NILES: Shades of orchid to purple three layer dress with chiffon sleeves, nude hose, orchid suede shoes, beaded headband, jewels

TERRY VIOLINO: Lt. green with reddish overstripe suit, dusty pink shirt, brick & cream tie, rust & white hankie, black belt, black sox, black shoes

DAVID EVANS: Brown tweed three-piece suit, lt. orange & white striped shirt, brown/orange/blue print tie, lt. brown hankie, brown shoes, brown belt, brown sox

SVETLANA MCLEE GRODY: Grey jersey dress lined with purple, ombre scarf, pearls, nude hose, brown shoes

MAVIS RAY: Peach & lavender print chiffon dress with attached scarf and feather trim, nude hose, nude shoes, jewelry

PETER GLADKE: Brown & cream suit, orange shirt, rust & green tie, brown belt, brown hankie, brown shoes, brown sox

RUDY TRONTO: Red mess jacket, black tux pants, white shirt, black bowtie, black hose, black sox

MARILYN COOPER: Purple print pleated chiffon dress, nude hose, beige chanel pumps, jewelry

DICK CORRIGAN: Rust/cream/blue plaid sport coat, beige & cream pants, orange, black tie, brown hankie, cream shirt, reddish shoes, sox

BUD FLEMING: Lt. green tweedy jacket, brown & green plaid pants, pink shirt, maroon belt, pinky hankie, mardon shoes, sox

CAROL FLEMMING: Rust with red print chiffon dress over orchid, red rose, nude hose, Burgundy shoes, jewelry

MICKEY GUNNERSEN: Pink/beige blue print taffeta dress over pink, with gold ruffles, Maroon shoes, nude hose, jewelry

ALFRED KARL: Brown & beige plaid coat, yellowish brown pants, green plaid shirt, green/orange tie, orangy hankie, brown argyle sox, brown shoes

DOROTHY LISTER: Rose & burgundy striped print chiffon dress over lavender, Beige hose, beige shoes, jewelry

JOHN J. MARTIN: Grey three piece suit, blue brown & white shirt, blue tie, black shoes, black sox

JOE MILAN: Green sport coat, green tweed pants, pink striped shirt, maroon/green tie, black belt, maroon hankie, brown shoes, pattern sox

FRANK PIETRIE: Brown/rust plaid jacket, rust pants, blue & beige belt, green shirt orange/brown/cream tie, avocado hankie, maroon shoes, sox

SALLY-JANE HEIT: Black sparkle sheer blouse with skirt from scene one.

DOROTHY DANNER: Grey & lavender print chiffon dress over orchid, silver shoes, sunglasses, jewelry

PETER ALZADO: Brown shiny suit, brown & cream striped shirt, yellow/beige tie, black shoes, black sox.

ACT ONE, SCENE 4—Living Room 1
DOROTHY LOUDON: Same as ACT ONE, SCENE 3
SALLY-JANE HEIT: Same as ACT ONE, SCENE 1 add brownish wrap sweater
JOHN HALLOW: Purple & blue striped pajamas; beige raincoat, camel hat, black shoes and sox

ACT ONE, SCENE 5—Ballroom 2—"The Tango"
DOROTHY LOUDON: Red silk dress with brown sheer overlay, matching pumps, nude hose, jewelry

VINCENT GARDENIA: Blue 3-piece suit, blue shirt, red tie, black shoes, black sox, red hankie

LYNN ROBERTS: Black sequin gown, silver sandals, nude hose, jewelry

BERNIE KNEE: Red brocade jacket, black tux pants, white shirt, red bow tie, black sox, black patent shoes

PATRICIA DRYLIE: Rust sparkle dress with black sheer overlay, yellow & green print shoes with gold trim, nude hose, jewelry

HOWARD PARKER: Gold & rust print velvet jacket, reddish brown pants, yellow & brown belt, pinky-red shirt, yellow & black print bow tie

BARBARA ERWIN: Black sparkly jumpsuit lined with red, orange brocade fringed sash, nude hose, red satin shoes with cross laces, jewelry

GENE KELTON: Red file jacket, black pants, lavender and navy shirt, red brocade bow tie, black & red shoes, black & white sox

LIZ SHERIDEN: Lavender sparkle dress with multi-bugle trim, red & gold brocade shoes, nude hose, beaded headband, jewelry

MICHAEL VITA: Purple & black brocade jacket, black pants striped with blue & violet, lavender ruffled shirt, red & navy tie, silver hankie, blue flower, navy & red patent shoes, maroon sox

JAYNE TURNER: Purple & gold lace & cut velvet dress, nude hose, purple shoes, jewelry

DANNY CARROLL: Maroon velvet jacket, black & grey striped dress pants, red & navy striped shirt, maroon velvet bow tie, red & black shoes, red sox

JANET WHITE: Turquoise, pink & gold brocade dress with black net overlay, nude hose, beige shoes, jewelry

ROBERTA HAZE: Blue fringed spanish shawl dress painted/red flowers, grey striped hose, purple shoes

VICTOR GRIFFIN: Gold print velvet jacket, maroon pants, hot pink and black print shirt, green ascot, gold hankie, maroon shoes, black sox

ADRIANA KEATHLEY: Purple & hot pink taffeta dress with black lace overlay, nude hose, magenta and gold shoes, rosette headpiece, jewelry

MARY ANN NILES: Orchid and turquoise taffeta dress with sparkle chiffon overlay, nude hose, black & gold brocade shoes, beaded headband, jewelry, glasses

TERRY VIOLINO: Green & black brocade jacket, reddish striped pants, black cummerbund, orchid ruffled shirt, black velvet bow tie, red & black shoes, maroon sox

DAVID EVANS: Green velvet suit, grey & black print shirt, green tie, red hankie, black shoes, dk. sox

SVETLANA MCLEE GRODY: Black & red cut velvet dress with black net ruffled trim, nude hose, black shoes, black point d'esprit hose, red headpiece, jewelry

MAVIS RAY: Red/green & black chiffon print dress with arm ruffles, nude hose, chartreuse and gold shoes, green headpiece, jewelry

PETER GLADKE: Red & black suit, rust striped shirt, maroon bow tie, black lizard shoes, maroon sox

RUDY TRONTO: Same as Ballroom 1

MARILYN COOPER: Green jersey dress, nude hose, magenta satin shoes

DICK CORRIGAN: Navy suit, red & white dotted shirt, navy tie, navy shoes & sox

BUD FLEMING: Green brocade jacket, black pants, grey shirt, black belt, red satin bow tie

CAROL FLEMMING: Turquoise dress with black & gold lace overlay, black hose, turquoise shoes, jewelry

MICKEY GUNNERSEN: Red & grey print taffeta dress, nude hose, red shoes, jewelry

ALFRED KARL: Bright blue & black brocade jacket, gold shirt, black pants, navy dotted tie, black shoes & sox

DOROTHY LISTER: Pink, black & green chiffon dress, nude hose, pink shoes, jewelry

JOHN J. MARTIN: Same as Ballroom 1

JOE MILAN: Red paisley jacket, black pants, black belt, pinkish rose shirt, maroon & white ascot, maroon & beige hankie, black shoes & sox

FRANK PIETRIE: Pink & black brocade jacket, black pants with grey fleck, blue shirt, red velvet bow tie, red hankie, black shoes & sox

SALLY-JANE HEIT: Same as Ballroom 1

DOROTHY DANNER: Blue & silver chiffon dress, silver shoes

PETER ALZADO: Same as Ballroom 1

ACT ONE, SCENE 6—Living Room 2
DOROTHY LOUDON: Same as Ballroom 2
VINCENT GARDENIA: Same as Ballroom 2

ACT ONE, SCENE 7—Junk Store 2
DOROTHY LOUDON: Blue & white print dress, nude hose, navy shoes, beige coat, brown purse

SALLY-JANE HEIT: Grey wrap skirt, grey/red/white striped blouse, nude hose, brown shoes

CAROL FLEMMING: Aqua 30's dress, nude hose, beige shoes

JAYNE TURNER: Pink sweater, rose pleated skirt, lavender print scarf, lavender shoes, nude hose

DOROTHY DANNER: Beige suit with brown overplaid, peach print blouse, nude hose, beige shoes, beige purse

ACT ONE, SCENE 8—Ballroom 3—"The Rhumba"

DOROTHY LOUDON: Orange silk wrap dress, matching shoes, nude hose, jewelry

VINCENT GARDENIA: Brown striped 3-piece suit, brown & white striped shirt, brown & beige tie, black shoes, black sox

LYNN ROBERTS: Grey pleated gown, gold & plastic shoes, nude hose, jewelry

BERNIE KNEE: Powder blue jacket, black pants, white tux shirt, black sox, black shoes

PATRICIA DRYLIE: Peach print wrap dress, beige shoes, nude hose, jewelry

HOWARD PARKER: Green/grey sport coat with beige overplaid, dk. beige pants, tan shirt, cream/beige/orange striped tie, camel belt, brown hankie, toning sox, brown suede shoes

BARBARA ERWIN: Peach chiffon dress, nude hose, bone shoes, jewelry

GENE KELTON: Cream sport coat with beige overplaid, grey/green pants, pink shirt, khaki & beige tie, red & white check belt, toning sox, camel & white shoes

LIZ SHERIDEN: White/purple/brown chiffon dress over lt. green nude hose, beige shoes, jewelry

MICHAEL VITA: Brown & blue mini-check jacket, camel pants, beige & brown striped shirt, blue & brown tie, lt. brown belt, brown & grey hankie, toning sox, brown suede shoes

JAYNE TURNER: White confetti print chiffon dress, nude hose, bluish shoes

DANNY CARROLL: Blue/cream/grey check suit, pink/blue/white plaid shirt, blue & red madras bow tie, grey belt, toning sox, brown shoes/tan

JANET WHITE: Blue chiffon dress, nude hose, beige shoes, jewelry

ROBERTA HAZE: Lavender & pink print dress, nude hose, purple shoes, jewels

VICTOR GRIFFIN: Grey & beige striped suit, beige shirt, beige & brown spotted tie, cream hankie, toning sox, tan shoes

ADRIANA KEATHLEY: Peach/cream/blue silk dress, nude hose, grey shoes, jewels

MARY ANN NILES: Beige print silk smocked dress with peach underslip, beige shoes, nude hose, jewels

TERRY VIOLINO: Lt. blue sport coat with peach overplaid, peach pants, lt. blue shirt with blue and peach stripes, brown belt, peach hankie, toning sox, brown shoes

DAVID EVANS: Grey/green/brown/blue plaid suit, cream shirt, green & brown tie, beige hankie, toning sox, brown shoes

SVETLANA MCLEE GRODY: Green/pink/white print dress with green & pink scarf, nude hose, bone shoes, jewelry

MAVIS RAY: White/green/beige print dress with matching scarf, nude hose, bone shoes, pearls

PETER GLADKE: Grey & blue striped suit, pink shirt, blue & cream tie, grey & brown hankie, lt. brown belt, toning sox, brown loafers

RUDY TRONTO: Grey mess jacket, black pants, white shirt, black bow tie, black sox, black shoes

MARILYN COOPER: Yellow print pleated chiffon dress, nude hose, yellow shoes, jewelry

DICK CORRIGAN: Blue & grey striped jacket, beige pants, yellow shirt, beige & blue tie, blue belt, beige & cream hankie, toning sox, lt. brown shoes

BUD FLEMING: Rust & cream patterned jacket, tan pants, beige shirt, rust & brown bow tie, beige & brown hankie, camel belt, toning sox, brown shoes

CAROL FLEMMING: Yellow & green print chiffon dress, nude hose, bone shoes, jewels

ALFRED KARL: Cream/blue/burgundy tweed jacket, brown pants, pink shirt, blue/cream/pink tie, brown belt, toning sox, brown shoes

MICKEY GUNNERSEN: Pink chiffon dress, nude hose, beige shoes

DOROTHY LISTER: Peach polka dot chiffon dress, nude hose, bone & brown shoes

JOHN J. MARTIN: Same as Ballroom 1

JOE MILAN: Burgundy & cream plaid jacket, lt. blue shirt, burgundy & cream striped pants, burgundy & blue paisley tie on cream, toning sox, reddish brown shoes

FRANK PIETRIE: Tan sport coat, grey & beige striped pants, blue striped shirt, cream & brown tie, grey hankie, toning sox, brown shoes

PETER ALZADO: Same as Ballroom 1

ACT ONE, SCENE 9—Living Room 3
DOROTHY LOUDON: Peach flowered penoir, tan slippers

VINCENT GARDENIA: Pants & shirt from Ballroom 3, brown tweed sports coat

SALLY-JANE HEIT: Grey wrap skirt, black/white/red check shirt, raincoat, purse, same hose & shoes

JOHN HALLOW: Grey pants, plaid shirt, beige raincoat, camel hat, black sox, brown shoes

ACT ONE, SCENE 10—Ballroom 4—"The Hustle"
DOROTHY LOUDON: Lavender silk wrap dress, matching shoes, nude hose, jewels

LYNN ROBERTS: Green sequined gown, gold shoes, nude hose

BERNIE KNEE: Red brocade jacket, black pants, white shirt, black bow tie, black sox, black shoes

PATRICIA DRYLIE: Copper silk chamuse, 2-piece dress, nude hose, copper shoes

HOWARD PARKER: Brown 2-piece suit, orange shirt, maroon hankie, brown & yellow belt, toning sox, tango shoes

BARBARA ERWIN: Black low waisted dress with red sash & burgundy petticoat, nude hose, red laced shoes

GENE KELTON: Maroon 3-piece suit, green shirt, red hankie, black & white sox, shoes from tango

LIZ SHERIDEN: Aubergine dress with red petticoat, nude hose, carmel patent shoes, rose embroidered headscarf

MICHAEL VITA: Navy blue suit, orange striped shirt, maroon tie, red & navy belt, toning sox, tango shoes

JAYNE TURNER: Purple 2-piece dress with textured pleated skirt, nude hose, red shoes

DANNY CARROLL: Bright green suit, orchid shirt, green & red dotted bow tie, black sox, tango shoes

JANET WHITE: Purple dress with velvet bodice & pink petticoat, nude hose, purple shoes

ROBERTA HAZE: Red dress with knit top and orange petticoat, nude hose, purple shoes, lavender choker

VICTOR GRIFFIN: Brown suit with self overplaid, purple shirt, olive knit tie, blue hankie, maroon sox, tango shoes

ADRIANA KEATHLEY: Rust & brick jersey dress with pink-red petticoat, nude hose, maroon shoes

MARY ANN NILES: Purple to red knit top, purple pleated skirt, deep red patent shoes, beaded headband, nude hose

TERRY VIOLINO: Rust suit, green shirt, brown belt, green hankie, maroon sox, tango shoes

DAVID EVANS: Maroon textured suit (3-piece), deep rose shirt, maroon tie, brown hankie, maroon sox, tango shoes

SVETLANA MCLEE GRODY: Purple dress with hot pink trim & lining, nude hose, black shoes, glitter pin

MAVIS RAY: Maroon dress with knit halter top, hot pink petticoat, nude hose, burgundy patent shoes

PETER GLADKE: Bright blue suit, tan shirt, orange tie, orange hankie, orange sox, tango shoes

RUDY TRONTO: Red mess jacket, black tux pants, white shirt, black bow tie, black shoes, black sox

MARILYN COOPER: Purple jersey wrap dress, nude hose, hot pink shoes

DICK CORRIGAN: Green suit, putty shirt, camel belt, green & rust tie, green & rust hankie, toning sox, tango shoes

BUD FLEMING: Blue suit, maroon shirt, black belt, blue hankie, black sox, tango shoes

CAROL FLEMMING: Maroon harlequin textured dress with orange-red petticoat, nude hose, maroon shoes

MICKEY GUNNERSEN: Purple dress with red petticoat & ruffles, red shoes, nude hose

ALFRED KARL: Olive green suit, mauve shirt, brown hankie, brown belt, green sox, tango shoes

DOROTHY LISTER: Deep rose & deep pink dress, nude hose, burgundy shoes

JOHN J. MARTIN: Same as Ballroom 2

JOE MILAN: Brown suit, fuchsia shirt, brown belt, maroon hankie, brown sox, tango shoes

FRANK PIETRIE: Bright blue suit, grey/lavender shirt, gold hankie, brown belt, black sox, black shoes

DOROTHY DANNER: Eggplant jersey dress with fuchsia petticoat & hip wrap, lavender cord necklace, nude hose, purple shoes

PETER ALZADO: Same as previous Ballrooms

ACT ONE, SCENE 11—Outside the Ballroom
DOROTHY LOUDON: Add off-white shawl & purse
VINCENT GARDENIA: Same as Ballroom 3
TERRY VIOLINO: Add brown raincoat
MARY ANN NILES: Add burgundy & gold shawl, lt. blue beaded bag
BARBARA ERWIN: Red & navy challis shawl, black beaded bag
ROBERTA HAZE: Add red & gold shawl, red purse
HOWARD PARKER: Add beige raincoat
PATRICIA DRYLIE: Add green raincoat, brown purse

ACT ONE, SCENE 12—Living Room 4

DOROTHY LOUDON: Same as Ballroom 4

SALLY-JANE HEIT: Green paisley dress with brick print & belt, nude hose, brown shoes, beige raincoat, brown purse

JOHN HALLOW: Grey pants, plaid shirt, beige raincoat, camel hat, black sox, brown shoes

DOROTHY DANNER: Peach pleated skirt, beige pointelle knit sweater, golden-brown silk blouse, nude hose, beige shoes

PETER ALZADO: Camel corduroy jacket, brown pants, brown belt, blue & bone shirt, khaki knit tie, black sox, brown desert boots

ACT ONE, SCENE 13—Ballroom 5—"The Waltz"

DOROTHY LOUDON: White peu d'soie beaded dress, with petticoat, nude hose, white shoes, rhinestones

VINCENT GARDENIA: Black 3-piece tuxedo, white shirt, black bow tie, suspenders, black sox, black patent shoes

LYNN ROBERTS: White beaded jersey gown, nude hose, silver sandals

BERNIE KNEE: Black tuxedo, white shirt, black bow tie, commerbund, black sox, black shoes

PATRICIA DRYLIE: White over peach gown with tigerlily trim, nude hose, peach shoes, headpiece

HOWARD PARKER: Black tuxedo, white shirt, black bow tie, cummerbund, black sox, black shoes

BARBARA ERWIN: White over yellow & blue handkerchief point gown trimmed with blue ostrich, nude hose, gold satin shoes

GENE KELTON: Black tuxedo, white shirt, black bow tie, cummerbund, black sox, black shoes

LIZ SHERIDEN: White over pink & green gown trimmed with beaded shawl, nude hose, grey shoes, pink headband

MICHAEL VITA: Black tuxedo, white shirt, black bow tie, cummerbund, black sox, black shoes

JAYNE TURNER: Grey & white over lavender gown with shoulder rosette, nude hose, grey suede shoes, headpiece

DANNY CARROLL: Black tuxedo, white shirt, black bow tie, cummerbund, black sox, black shoes

JANET WHITE: White/lavender satin gown with beaded bodice and lavender beaded skirt, nude hose, beige shoes

ROBERTA HAZE: White over peach/rose pleated gown with diamante straps, nude hose, grey suede shoes, headpiece

VICTOR GRIFFIN: Black tuxedo, white shirt, cummerbund, black bow tie, black sox, black shoes

ADRIANA KEATHLEY: White over aqua gown trimmed with lace and silk flowers, nude hose, grey shoes, headpiece

MARY ANN NILES: White lace over orchid chiffon gown, trimmed with orchid sash, orchid shoes, nude hose, beaded headband

TERRY VIOLINO: Black tuxedo, white shirt, black bow tie, cummerbund, black sox, black shoes

DAVID EVANS: Black tuxedo, white shirt, black bow tie, cummerbund, black sox, black shoes

SVETLANA MCLEE GRODY: White over grey & blue gown, nude hose, cream shoes, flower wreath

MAVIS RAY: White over pink & grey gown trimmed with pink & grey ostrich, nude hose, white shoes

PETER GLADKE: Black tuxedo, white shirt, black bow tie, cummerbund, black sox, black shoes

RUDY TRONTO: Black tuxedo, white shirt, black bow tie, cummerbund, black sox, black shoes

MARILYN COOPER: White over aqua & pink with capelet, nude hose, white shoes

DICK CORRIGAN: Black tuxedo, white shirt, black bow tie, cummerbund, black sox, black shoes

BUD FLEMING: Black tuxedo, white shirt, black bow tie, cummerbund, black sox, black shoes

CAROL FLEMMING: White lace over blue, with sparkle sheer cummerbund, nude hose, beige shoes, headpiece

MICKEY GUNNERSEN: White over peach gown trimmed with silk roses, nude hose, beige shoes, headpiece

ALFRED KARL: Black tuxedo, white shirt, black bow tie, cummerbund, black shoes, black sox

DOROTHY LISTER: White over pink/blue/yellow gown with pink sash, nude hose, bone shoes, headpiece

JOHN J. MARTIN: Black tuxedo, white shirt, black bow tie, cummerbund, black shoes, black sox

JOE MILAN: Black tuxedo, white shirt, black bow tie, cummerbund, black sox, black shoes

FRANK PIETRIE: Black tuxedo, white shirt, black bow tie, cummerbund, black sox, black shoes

SALLY-JANE HEIT: White beaded gown over peach slip, white belt, nude hose, white shoes

DOROTHY DANNER: White silk blouse, white silk skirt, silver beaded belt, nude hose, bone shoes.

PETER ALZADO: Black 3-piece tuxedo, white shirt, black bow tie, black sox, black shoes

JOHN HALLOW: Black tuxedo, white shirt, black bow tie, cummerbund, black sox and shoes

DRESSER

7:00 PM PRE-SET
Stage Right
Helen's raincoat and purse in junk shop: coat on rack, purse on second hook.
Lynn Roberts' tango dress and jewels upstage near winch.

Stage Left
Flemming Rhumba shoes and jewels, Jane Turner's Rhumba jewels, Erwin's Foxtrot shoes and jewels on back winches, three dresses (*Erwin's foxtrot, Carol and Jane's Rhumba*) on back hooks.
Coat Room: Drylie's wool coat and Dottie Lister's shawl on hooks.
Give Dottie Frank's brown jacket and Erwin's Boa to props.

8:00 PM SHOWTIME
Barbara Erwin's quick change:
—get raincoat from David Evans and fur from Svetlana.
—wait for Barbara to come back to adjust shoes.
Strike clothes and raincoat and fur.
Go to stage left and pick up 3 or 4 raincoats and shawls depending on who is in the show. Leave them on the stage left winch.
Bring those coats to coat-room, stage left.
At the end of "Dreams" go to stage right and change Lynn Roberts.
Strike Lynn's clothing.
Pick up Drylie's green raincoat and brown purse, Howard Parker's raincoat, Dorothy Loudon's white shawl and purse, and pre-set them on the stage right winch. Also pick up Roberta Haze's shawl and purse (*Hustle costume*) and Barbara Erwin's shawl and purse (*Hustle costume*) and pre-set on hooks near winch stage right.
Go upstairs (*Stage Left*) at the beginning of Living Room 1 with Mary Ann Niles' Hustle purse and shawl and basket. Pre-set shawl and purse in coat-room along with Terry Violino's coat which should be hanging in the coat-room. (*If it is not it will be downstairs*) Put any extra coats in basket, take to the winch and set up for Rhumba change.
Change Carol Flemming into Rhumba and assist in Dorothy Loudon's change.
Strike Dorothy's clothes to dressing room.
Stage right-set up for Dorothy's change.
Stage right-assist in Dorothy's change-before Living Room 3.
Pre-set Roberta Haze and Erwin's shawls and purses on right banquette.
Assist in Dorothy's change, strike robe and slippers to Dorothy's dressing room.
Give coats and shawl and purses to Peter Gladke post Hustle scene. Stand at Rudy's bar. He will come out at the Nomination of Bea Asher.
    Assist during Waltz change for Dorothy.
Strike Dorothy's clothes to dressing room.

PROPERTY LIST

Stage Right Checklist
Cold Compresses, Kleenex, Water Cups
hat palate-antique vase-jewelry box
Daughter's Brown Purse and Blue Dress
Black Purse with money, One Men's wallet with money
Scrabble Set with two trays set up, pad and pencil
    Tiles in top of box (*NB-see separate sheet*)
Plate with coffee cake and knife
Winner's envelope (*with insert*)

Counter (Junk) R1
TOP: Telephone, fan palate, crystal palate with 1 loose glass, check book, bills, pen, receipt book, scotch tape holder, black palate.
INSIDE: mortise (lower shelf) Cash box with change, $$$ bills, receipt book, pencil
ON HOOKS: Helen's purse (L.), Bea's purse (R.)

UNDER: Newspaper (1 large sheet)
HANGER: Helen's coat on loose hanger (2nd from R.)
FLAT: Boat set at C.

Living Room R2
COFFEE TABLE: Candy Dish, Bea's clutch bag, Jewelry box
SOFA: Afghan (One corner folded) (down C)-Bea's Coat
SIDEBOARD: 4 candle holders, 4 picture frames, fruit bowl (C.), telephone
    (D.S. Edge), Dictionary in U.S. Drawer.

M.R. Table
Pad, pencil, towels, 18 glasses, 1 lg. bull glass with liquid (V8) and celery stick,
    bottle of drinking water with 4 clean glasses.

U.R. Table
Silver Coffee Pot with Milk, sugar bowl, 2 cups and saucers, 2 napkins, 2 spoons
    on silver tray

U.R. Living Room
Bookcase with radio and dictionary (Mortise around books)

Stage Right Ballroom Platform (Pre-set)
2 tables
D.S. TABLE: 1 ashtray with water (attached), clipboard.
U.S. TABLE: cigarettes and matches (J. Martin), ashtray with water.
BAR: 1 martini, 1 glass water, ashtray with water, cigarettes with matches, 1 bar
    towel, six chairs on spike

Bandstand
2 chairs on spike
D.C. stand mike with hand mike coiled L. of C. on rise.
Silver trophy (O.R. edge) O.S.R. on rise
Bronze trophy a/a
marachas on rise R. of C.
Clavas on rise L. of C.

ELECTRICS—U.S. dressing room lites 1 off on individual switch, 2 on with blue
    gell

Personal—5 file cards with pencils, Tango judges, 4 purses (Marilyn Cooper,
    Dottie Frank, Barbara Erwin, R. Haze), 1 winner's envelope with insert
    (Bernie Knee)

Stage Left Checklist
PROP TABLE
1 bar tray with 3 glasses (2 champagne, 1 beer)
Martha's purse with money
1 diet paper-G.K.

1 Emily's notes-J.M.
1 cardboard container (2 hard paper plates, taped) with fake cottage cheese, let-tuce, 3 lemons, fork inside.
1 Chinese food container, 1 highball glass, 1 purple dress, 2 hats, sweater, purse, cold compresses
Pitcher of water with cups
Diane's brown velvet jacket (wardrobe)

CHECK ROOM on hooks: Pat Drylie's coat (wardrobe), a/a Dorothy Lister's shawl a/a

BALLROOM PLATFORM: 6 chairs on spike

JUNK:
Check-Make sure the "DOG" is in.
Mannequin with blue dress and scarf facing D.L. corner
Indian Headdress on headblock at D.R. corner
large white picture hat on D.S. edge of mirror
grey hat and sweater on standing hanger D.L. Corner

LIVING ROOM: 2 or 3 umbrellas fixed into umbrella stand

ELECTRICS: Radio control on lamp turned *ON* (on bottom shelf of lamp table)

PROPERTY MOVES

Stage Right
ACT ONE, SCENE 1
Strike/Move
HOLD—sideboard and palate off to side.
Set
Jewelry box on coffee table: COUNTER in place; TOP—phone, fan palate, crystal palate, check book, receipt book with pen, scotch tape dispenser, black palate (R. to L.); INSIDE—(top shelf) cash box, with money, receipt book, pencil; ON HOOKS—Offstage—Bea's purse, onstage—Helen's Purse; UNDER (at Center)—one large sheet of newspaper; BACK HANGER—(2nd from R.) Helen's coat on loose hanger; ON JUNK FLAT CENTER—Pink feather Boa

ACT ONE, SCENE 2
Strike/Move
MOVE—*Junk counter* D.S. After street people are on. Set-up PALATE and SIDEBOARD for *Living Room*
Set
STREET SCENE I—Wallet with money (Victor Griffin)

ACT ONE, SCENE 3
Strike/Move
JUNK I—countertop; Strike—crystal palate, check book, bills with paper, pen,

lunch; Strike—hat palate, blue dress, brown purse, black purse with money, antique vase. Move—phone between fan palate (1st) and hat palate REST ARE STET; DURING BALLROOM I: Tray—Bill; Clipboard—Pauline

Set

BALLROOM I

OFF M.R. TABLE—1 lg. glass with liquid and celery stick. 18 glasses, bottle of water towels, pad, pencil. BAR—2 glasses, cigarettes, matches ashtray and water; U.S. TABLE—cigarettes and matches ashtray with water; D.S. TABLE—Clipboard with pencil, ashtray with water

ACT ONE, Scene 4

Set

LIVING ROOM I—Sideboard set up; afghan on couch-folded; candy dish on coffee table; dictionary on U.R. bookcase

ACT ONE, Scenes 5 & 6

Strike/Move

LIVING ROOM I—ALL PROPS STET; DURING BALLROOM II—Bronze Trophy-R1-(DE & SG)

Set

BALLROOM II—Bronze Trophy—Bandstand; Silver Trophy—Bandstand

ACT ONE, Scene 7

Strike/Move

SET JUNK COUNTER

Set

LIVING ROOM II—All props stet; U.R. Table—coffee service with 2 spoons, and napkins

ACT ONE, Scene 8

Strike/Move

Strike—2 Center bandstand chairs to under orch. Mike stand to under band platform; Leave-mike; LIVING ROOM II:-Strike—sideboard & palates, candy dish, fruit bowl; Move—coffee service from coffee table to sideboard. Coffee cake plate with knife to U.R. Table; Set—scrabble set with lid with tile on top to coffee table

JUNK II

Brown Purse with blue dress (C)

Black purse with money

antique vase

hat palate

ACT ONE, Scene 9

Strike/Move

JUNK II: Move—counter D.S.; Re-set living room sideboard

Set

BALLROOM III

ACT ONE, Scene 10

Set

LIMBO

ACT ONE, SCENE 11
Set
LIVING ROOM III—Scrabble set on coffee table; U.R. Table—plate with cake
    & knife

ACT ONE, SCENE 12
Strike/Move
LIVING ROOM III: STRIKE—coffee service from sideboard, scrabble from
    coffee table, scrabble lid from sofa, coffee cake from sideboard; RE-SET
    candy dish on coffee table, fruit bowl on sideboard
Set
BALLROOM IV—Tray with glasses, pad, pen

ACT ONE, SCENE 13
Set
STREET SCENE II

ACT ONE, SCENE 14
Set
LIVING ROOM IV—All props back to original set-up

ACT ONE, SCENE 15
Strike/Move
LIVING ROOM IV: MOVE—coffee table off palate to side
Set
BALLROOM V—Winner's envelope with insert

Stage Left
ACT ONE, SCENE 1
Strike/Move
Martha's purse; Boa in newspaper-repeats; JUNK-change dress to purple, strike
    jewelry box; change hat on mirror to purse; change feathers to hat; change
    grey hat and sweater to red hat and white sweater; wallet—Al
Set
JUNK I—Martha's purse with money; Lunch with fork (Angie)

ACT ONE, SCENE 2
Set
STREET—Diet paper (Petey); Boa (Martha)

ACT ONE, SCENE 3
Strike/Move
Receive Bea's coat and purse—set on Umbrella Stand (coat on D.S. hook purse
    on shelf)
Set
BALLROOM I—Tray with 5 glasses; highball glass (J.J.M.)

ACT ONE, SCENE 4
Set
LIVING ROOM I—Bea's purse and coat on umbrella stand

ACT ONE, SCENES 5 & 6
Strike/Move
Silver Trophy—Shirley and Paul
Set
BALLROOM II

ACT ONE, SCENE 7
Set
LIVING ROOM II

ACT ONE, SCENE 8
Strike/Move
2 purses and blue dress
Set
JUNK II—Strike chairs from bandstand

ACT ONE, SCENE 9
Set
BALLROOM III

ACT ONE, SCENE 10
Set
LIMBO

ACT ONE, SCENE 11
Strike/Move
Chinese food—Helen; receive Jack's coat Helen coat & bag
Set
LIVING ROOM III: Purse—Helen; Chink food—Helen; Al's jacket on chair

ACT ONE, SCENE 12
Strike/Move
LIVING ROOM III—Diane's coat on D.S. hook on umbrella stand; Helen's coat
    on purse on U.S. hook on stand; Jack's coat on middle hook on stand;
    Strike—Al's coat from chair; ELEC—TURN LAMP CONTROL OFF
Set
BALLROOM IV
Emily's note-J. Milan

ACT ONE, SCENE 13
Set
STREET

ACT ONE, SCENE 14
Set
LIVING ROOM IV
Clothes set on umbrella stand

ACT ONE, SCENE 15
Set
BALLROOM V

SCRABBLE SET-UP STAGE RIGHT

2 tile trays with magnetic strip on the back.
Letters used are also backed with magnetic strip

Vinnie's G U L L A B E (plays up stage) on coffee table
Dorothy's R T S T R O T (plays D. stage) on coffee table
ALL TILES IN LID OF BOX TURNED FACE DOWN
IN LID OF BOX—pre-set separately face down with magnetic strip on back col-
    or coded
red—A D O R A
yellow—F X S
no color—3 blanks
Board set C of coffee table with B I L E glued onto board going vertically down
    C L on C slot
The game is written out on the board

```
              A
              D
        F O X T R O T S
              R
              A
              B
        R     I
G U L L A B L E
        T     E
        S
```

NEW

BROADWAY COMEDIES

from

SAMUEL FRENCH, INC.

DIVISION STREET – DOGG'S HAMLET,
CAHOOT'S MACBETH – FOOLS – GOREY
STORIES – GROWNUPS – I OUGHT TO BE IN
PICTURES – IT HAD TO BE YOU – JOHNNY
ON A SPOT – THE KINGFISHER – A LIFE –
LOOSE ENDS – LUNCH HOUR – MURDER AT
THE HOWARD JOHNSON'S – NIGHT AND DAY –
ONCE A CATHOLIC – ROMANTIC COMEDY –
ROSE – SPECIAL OCCASIONS – THE SUICIDE
– THE SUPPORTING CAST – WALLY'S CAFE

For descriptions of plays, consult our free Basic Catalogue of Plays.

Other Publications for Your Interest

COMING ATTRACTIONS
(ADVANCED GROUPS—COMEDY WITH MUSIC)

By TED TALLY, music by JACK FELDMAN, lyrics by BRUCE SUSSMAN and FELDMAN

5 men, 2 women—Unit Set

Lonnie Wayne Burke has the requisite viciousness to be a media celebrity—but he lacks vision. When we meet him, he is holding only four people hostage in a laundromat. There aren't any cops much less reporters around, because they're across town where some guy is holding 50 hostages. But, a talent agent named Manny sees possibilities in Lonnie Wayne. He devises a criminal persona for him by dressing him in a skeleton costume and sending him door-to-door, murdering people as "The Hallowe'en Killer". He is captured, and becomes an instant celebrity, performing on TV shows. When his fame starts to wane, he crashes the Miss America Pageant disguised as Miss Wyoming to kill Miss America on camera. However, he falls in love with her, and this eventually leads to his downfall. Lonnie ends up in the electric chair, and is fried "live" on prime-time TV as part of a jazzy production number! "Fizzles with pixilated laughter."—Time. "I don't often burst into gales of laughter in the theatre; here, I found myself rocking with guffaws."—New York Mag. "Vastly entertaining."—Newark Star-Ledger.

(Royalty, $50-$40.)

SORROWS OF STEPHEN
(ADVANCED GROUPS—COMEDY)

By PETER PARNELL

4 men, 5 women—Unit set

Stephen Hurt is a headstrong, impetuous young man—an irrepressible romantic—he's unable not to be in love. One of his models is Goethe's tragic hero, Werther, but as a contemporary New Yorker, he's adaptable. The end of an apparently undying love is followed by the birth of a grand new passion. And as he believes there's a literary precedent for all romantic possibilities justifying his choices—so with enthusiasm bordering on fickleness, he turns from Tolstoy, to Stendhal or Balzac. And Stephen's never discouraged—he can withstand rivers of rejection. (From the N.Y. Times.) And so his affairs—real and tentative—begin when his girl friend leaves him. He makes a romantic stab at a female cab driver, passes an assignation note to an unknown lady at the opera, flirts with an accessible waitress—and then has a tragic-with-comic-overtones, wild affair with his best friend's fiancée. "Breezy and buoyant. A real romantic comedy, sophisticated and sentimental, with an ageless attitude toward the power of positive love."—N.Y. Times.

(Slightly Restricted. Royalty, $50-$40, where available)

The Gingerbread Lady

NEIL SIMON
(Little Theatre) Comedy-Drama
3 Men, 3 Women—Interior

Maureen Stapleton played the Broadway part of a popular singer who has gone to pot with booze and sex. We meet her at the end of a ten-week drying out period at a sanitarium, when her friend, her daughter, and an actor try to help her adjust to sobriety. But all three have the opposite effect on her. The friend is so constantly vain she loses her husband; the actor, a homosexual, is also doomed, and indeed loses his part three days before an opening; and the daughter needs more affection than she can spare her mother. Enter also a former lover louse, who ends up giving her a black eye. The birthday party washes out, the gingerbread lady falls off the wagon and careens onward to her own tragic end.

"He has combined an amusing comedy with the atmosphere of great sadness. His characteristic wit and humor are at their brilliant best, and his serious story of lost misfits can often be genuinely and deeply touching."—N.Y. Post. "Contains some of the brightest dialogue Simon has yet composed."—N.Y. Daily News. "Mr. Simon's play is as funny as ever—the customary avalanche of hilarity, and landslide of pure unbuttoned joy . . . Mr. Simon is a funny, funny man—with tears running down his cheek."—N.Y. Times.

Royalty $50-$35

The Sunshine Boys

NEIL SIMON
(All Groups) Comedy
5 Men, 2 Women

An ex-vaudeville team, Al Lewis and Willie Clarke, in spite of playing together for forty-three years, have a natural antipathy for one another. (Willie resents Al's habit of poking a finger in his chest, or perhaps accidentally spitting in his face). It has been eleven years since they have performed together, when along comes CBS-TV, who is preparing a "History of Comedy" special, that will of course include Willie and Al—the "Lewis and Clark" team back together again. In the meantime, Willie has been doing spot commercials, like for Schick (the razor blade shakes) or for Frito-Lay potato chips (he forgets the name), while Al is happily retired. The team gets back together again, only to have Al poke his finger in Willie's chest, and accidentally spit in his face.

". . . the most delightful play Mr. Simon has written for several seasons and proves why he is the ablest current author of stage humor."—Watts, N. Y. Post. "None of Simon's comedies has been more intimately written out of love and a bone-deep affinity with the theatrical scene and temperament." Time. ". . . another hit for Neil Simon in this shrewdly balanced, splendidly performed and rather touching slice of the show-biz life."—Watt, New York Daily News. "(Simon) . . . writes the most dependably crisp and funny dialogue around . . . always well-set and polished to a high lustre."—WABC-TV. ". . . a vaudeville act within a vaudeville act . . . Simon has done it again."—WCBS-TV.

Royalty $50-$35

Other Publications for Your Interest

VIVIEN
(COMIC DRAMA)
By PERCY GRANGER

2 men, 1 woman—Unit set

Recently staged to acclaim at Lincoln Center, this lovely piece is about a young stage director who visits his long-lost father in a nursing home and takes him to see a production of "The Seagull" that he staged. Along the way, each reveals a substantial truth about himself, and the journey eventually reaches, its zenith in a restaurant after the performance. "A revealing father-son portrait that gives additional certification to the author's position as a very original playwright."—N.Y. Times. "The dialogue has the accuracy of real people talking."—N.Y. Post.

(Royalty, $15–$10.)

LANDSCAPE WITH WAITRESS
(COMEDY)
By ROBERT PINE

1 man, 1 woman—Interior

Arthur Granger is an unsuccessful novelist who lives a Walter Mitty-like fantasy existence. Tonight, he is dining out in an Italian restaurant which seems to have only one waitress and one customer—himself. As Arthur selects his dinner he has fantasies of romantic conquest, which he confides to the audience and to his notebook. While Arthur's fantasies take him into far-fetched plots, the waitress acts out the various characters in his fantasy. Soon, Arthur is chattering and dreaming away at such a quick clip that neither he nor we can be entirely sure of his sanity. Arthur finishes his dinner and goes home, ending as he began—as a lover *manqué*. " . . . a landscape of the mind."—Other Stages. " . . . has moments of true originality and a bizarre sense of humor . . . a devious and slightly demented half-hour of comedy."—N.Y. Times. Recently a hit at New York's excellent Ensemble Studio Theatre.

(Royalty, $15–$10.)

NEW MUSICALS

from

SAMUEL FRENCH, INC.

BALLROOM – THE BEST LITTLE WHOREHOUSE
IN TEXAS – CHICAGO – CHRISTMAS IS COMIN'
UPTOWN – THE CLUB – COLE – THE DRACULA
SPECTACULAR – DRACULA: THE *MUSICAL?* –
FESTIVAL – THE FIRST – GOLD DUST –
HAPPY END – HAPPY NEW YEAR – HIJINKS! –
A HISTORY OF THE AMERICAN FILM – I LOVE MY
WIFE – I'M GETTING MY ACT TOGETHER AND
TAKING IT ON THE ROAD – JERRY'S GIRLS –
KURT VONNEGUT'S GOD BLESS YOU MR.
ROSEWATER – MARCH OF THE FALSETTOS –
MUSICAL CHAIRS – MY OLD FRIENDS –
THE 1940'S RADIO HOUR – OH, BROTHER!
ON THE TWENTIETH CENTURY – OPERETTA –
PETTICOAT LANE – PIAF – PIANO BAR –
THE PICTURE OF DORIAN GRAY – PUMP BOYS
AND DINETTES – THE ROCKY HORROR SHOW –
RUNAWAYS – THE SALOONKEEPER'S DAUGHTER –
THE SEVEN – STRIDER – SUGAR BABIES –
THEY'RE PLAYING OUR SONG – TRIXIE TRUE,
TEEN DETECTIVE – UNSUNG COLE (AND
CLASSICS, TOO) – THE UTTER GLORY OF
MORRISSEY HALL – THE WIZ – WOMAN
OVERBOARD – YOU NEVER KNOW

*For descriptions of these and all our musicals consult our Musicals
Catalogue, available FREE.*

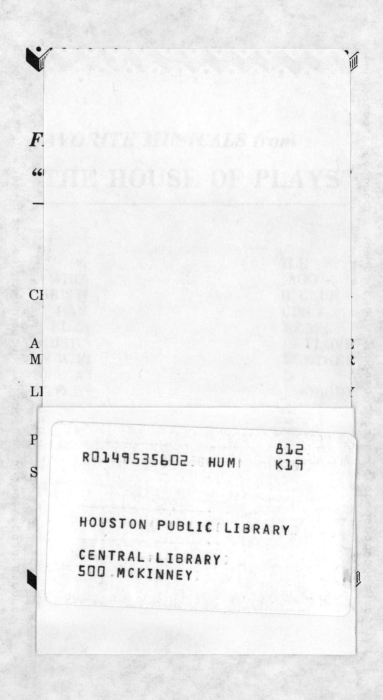